The Unknown Elf

KARLIE LUCAS

DEDICATION

To my amazing husband who helped me figure out the logistics and choreography necessary for my characters' various encounters. And to all my friends and family who believed in me even when I didn't.

ACKNOWLEDGMENTS

I would like to offer thanks to all my BETA readers, Gina Hintz Bacalski, Walter Bockemehl, and Daniel Lucas. Their input helped shape this story into what it is now. Also, a big thank you to Deborah Jackson for editing my manuscript until it bled ink.

PREFACE

IT WAS DIFFICULT to wait, wondering if they had discovered her as she crouched at the bottom of the stairs. Her muscles tensed as she listened, heart pounding in her ears. But the sound didn't come again. Perhaps it had only been residual thunder echoing across the sky. Then again, maybe not.

Taking a deep breath, she stepped onto the first riser, and waited. Nothing. No sound at all. At least nothing outside of the incessant drum of rain on steel, and the occasional drip from the pipes in the room behind her. The drops sent off a light ping as they hit the water, echoing in the cement cavity they'd called a room.

Tiptoeing, she let out her held breath and proceeded upwards. It was quiet in the dark. Too quiet. Pausing a few steps before the landing, she looked around. Trying to decide which way to go, she rubbed bleeding hands on torn, mud-covered pants.

Crates lay everywhere, with who knew what inside them. They were stacked from floor to ceiling, leaving only narrow corridors around the swaying stairs. Puddles of collected rainwater fell into empty rivet holes in the floor. She wished she dared lean against the rusted railing nearby.

Age and misuse had twisted the metal. Some spots were so bad that a spider's touch would likely make them dissolve into a fine red powder. The railing didn't seem like it would support much weight, but there was no choice. Not if she was going to escape. Besides, she was small and pretty flexible. The last stretch, the empty stair, wouldn't last long.

She placed a hand on the tortured metal, but immediately drew it back. There was a sound, a click. She stopped breathing, despite her heart pounding like a bass drum. Someone was coming, but she wasn't sure if it was one of her uncle's cronies, or if it was her uncle. It didn't matter though. She couldn't stop, not now that she was so close. Taking another breath, she lunged past the missing step and made the landing.

Choosing a right hand passage, she slipped into the labyrinth of crates. All the while, she tried to control lungs that wanted to work like over used billows. She welcomed the near silence her bare feet left, even if it meant the slightest of bloody footprints remained behind. At least the constant downpour from above hid the slight sound.

A joist groaned from the unaccustomed strain placed on it. Bright light suddenly shown down from the huge steel girders that held up the roof as lightning arced across the sky. One of the giant fans began to whine as it tried to spin into life. The sudden breeze hit her face, bringing with it the scent of a particular brand of cologne. She knew that fragrance all too well, that awful, sickening smell.

Her heart almost stopped as she realized it would be next to suicide to keep going in that direction. To do so meant only one thing, that she'd accepted the end of this little game, this feeble attempt at freedom. It meant that everything she'd worked so hard for wasn't worth anything. And that her life was meaningless. Just like he kept telling her. She would not, could not, go back to that. Instead, she started to run, knowing that it was the only other course open to her, the only chance that her plan might succeed.

She saw another flight of stairs, one that led to the upper levels of the building. Making a desperate choice, she decided to use them, regardless of where they might lead her. Abandoning all caution, she broke cover. Bounding upward, she grabbed hold of the railing for balance, somehow managing to avoid slipping on the wet surface. It was almost as if a small stream of water came from the poorly drained roof. Speed was the only thing that could save her now.

He smiled from his position, hidden among the crates, realizing that her abandonment of caution tipped favor's hand in his direction. He signaled for his men to corner her off as he closed in for the kill. The thrill of the hunt rang in his veins. Taking a moment to load the gun clip, he made sure to release the safety. One way or another, it would end tonight. Either he would have his revenge, or he'd at least find a satisfying end to yet another tool. It didn't matter which. After all, there were other means and ways to reach his goal.

Panting and gasping for breath, she lunged at the steps, higher and higher until there was none left. There was only a hallway with dim lighting at the top. Smaller rooms branched off on either side. She ran down the corridor to the door at the end, hoping it was unlocked.

He was behind her by only a few stairs, sure there would be no escape. Even now, the rest of his men were dispersing around the building, inside and out. There would be no escape tonight, or any night, for that matter. He reached the last step and slowed to a walk, knowing there was nowhere for her to go, no place she could hide.

She wrenched on the knob, only to find it locked, and almost cried out in frustration. Fortunately, she remembered some of the things she'd been forced to do before this crazy plan had come into being. Relaxing her mind, she sent tendrils of thought outwards, coaxing the door open with her mind. Tumblers shifted and gears moved at her mental command. The door opened and she ran through onto the roof.

Rocks bit at bare feet as she stepped out onto the roof, smudges of tar clinging to raw skin. She didn't even think about the pain; it was all she knew anyway. Rain made everything more slick than normal. It took just about every ounce of her concentration to not go skidding over to one of the high skylights. She didn't want to crash through the glass to a certain death.

He followed her outside. His eyes were almost black, like some feral animal, breath coming out in pants like a dog. There was nowhere for her to go and they both knew it, unless she jumped. She wouldn't though. It was instant death. And even though he knew he'd put her through hell, there was no way she'd do something like that.

The abrupt ending of the roof was too close for comfort. She backpedaled and waved her arms as she tried to not fall over the edge. It was a long way down, several stories or more. And with a dirt landing that was usually as hard as cement, it was definitely not the best option. Thankfully, there was a ladder further down, if she could get to it.

"Don't even think about it," he said, reading the direction of her body movement. He noted the presence of the fire ladder from the corner of his eye. "You'll be dead before you get there. Just come back this way, nice and easy. Come back to your room and I'll forget all this ever happened." He held the gun with one hand, steadying it with the other. All he had to do was squeeze the trigger.

"No!" she yelled in defiance as thunder cracked around them. Rain streamed down her filthy flesh and unwashed hair. "I'm not going back to that. I won't be your prisoner. You won't use me any more!" She trembled all over, remembering all the things she'd been forced to do. All the things that had happened since her parents had disappeared. "I'd rather die!"

"Fine." He brought the gun to bear as she ran towards

the ladder and fired. Lightning lit up the sky with the sudden flash of ignited powder. It filled the night with an almost overwhelming intensity as the bullet sped from the chamber of the handgun.

The bullet struck just left of her chest, near the shoulder blade. She lost balance, twisting from the force. With eyes wide open in shock, she stared at the man who had taken everything away, her freedom, her family, and now, her life. Her feet continued to twist as her head whipped around, sending her over the roof's edge as thunder rumbled through the air. A scream of agony was forced through frozen lips, and then was silenced as the rain came pouring down.

ONE

DRIFTS OF THICK, midnight lace sifted in the arctic winds of the North Polar Region. These winds threw the delicate bits of frozen filigree like torn fragments of spider silk. They dusted everything in sight, finishing a delayed spring-cleaning. Dark clouds hung low, barely letting in a pale-blue light. The moon hid inside its fairy ring in the only real opening in the sky. A few stars peeped through the cracks, hoping to catch the delicate sheen of the winter lace.

An elf walked across the barren, windswept trail. His long hair tried, without success, to escape the hood where his face shown a light red near high cheekbones. Deep, chocolate brown eyes reflected the night sky. He stared out, contemplating the darker blue shadows of the frozen wasteland. Clarence shivered. The night was colder than usual, not that it bothered him. He was far too familiar with the cold.

His gaze swept over the landscape, thoughts turning to his last errand. It was something someone else could have dealt with, but the timing couldn't have been more perfect. It had been some time since he'd last left North Pole City. His duties had made it almost impossible since even before last Christmas. Unfortunately, what was supposed to be a relatively pleasant escape had been a more complex event than what he'd first anticipated. One of the Observer Stations in Central Canada had been compromised. Fortunately, nothing seemed to have gone missing. None of the data appeared to be touched, at least as far as anyone could tell. But none of the testimonies quite matched any of the others.

Some claimed the intruder was male, others were adamant of it being female. None of the facts added up, and it made Clarence's head ache just to think about the matter. The most worrisome point was that this intruder, whoever he or she was, hadn't been detected on any of their scans or cameras. Whoever this person was had blended into their environment in such a manner that it was uncanny. Some were even blaming the strange phenomenon on a ghost, or, worse, saying that it was one of their own gone rogue.

Somehow, he'd managed to smooth things over, promising to send more elves from The Security League. He made a mental note to talk to Dena about that upon arriving back at headquarters. He didn't relish the idea of having to admit he had no idea what was going on, or who had found their way into the underground facility. All he had going for him were the reports of unease, of people seeing someone who shouldn't have been there. But with no proof, he wasn't sure how much Dena's people could do about the whole fiasco. Maybe it was just some kind of witch-hunt, though other incidents of similar nature negated that fact. It was not the first such incident of the New Year.

Clarence could have been home right now, warming himself by the giant fireplace in the Main Rotunda. He'd planned on doing just that, but something had made him take the long walk across the plains instead of using the Subway. He didn't know why but it just felt right to walk. He also felt the need to think through all of the recent developments. If reports were true, it could mean a lot of trouble for them all. There was nothing stopping someone from finding his or her way to this secluded chunk of ice. Especially not if that person had enough determination. It would not have been the first time someone had tried, or succeeded. It didn't bode well to think about the one time someone had succeeded.

The elf hugged his long coat around his body. A sudden strong gust of wind tried to swipe his hood in a mad game of hide and sneak, breaking his train of thought. He batted at the wind, trying to make it go away, but his efforts only seemed to add to its frenzy. It came back with more force, pushing the clouds until they blocked out the moon and stars completely.

After a while, he gave up at scolding. Instead, he tried to push his way through the rough splintering of ice crystals thrown up against him. The strong breeze had other ideas and would not let him move in any direction. It howled, rising with the sound of thunder, and forced him to the ground. It brought with it a faint echo of a voice.

The sound seemed to call out to him, rising in intensity and dying with each gust. The hopeless appeal caught his attention, sounding like the call of someone lost and afraid. It took him back to a day he didn't want to remember. It was the day when his so called friends had left him to wander out in the cold, without food or shelter to help him.

It had been a prank, one gone horribly wrong, and he'd been the object of it all. It wasn't his fault he'd been smarter as a child, quicker to pick up on things. Of course, his peers hadn't seen it that way, preferring to believe that he was only showing off to make them look bad. And he'd thought they were his friends! How wrong he'd been, realizing they'd tricked him and left him out on the tundra with nothing but the clothes on his back. Never again, he'd vowed. Never again.

Thinking back on that incident, he no longer found the

desire to try fighting. The call had struck a small part of his heart he hadn't realized was still there. It was filled with the innocence of youth. It was the voice of a child afraid of the dark that couldn't help but call out, hoping that someone would come to the rescue. He gingerly stood and followed the insistent tug of the wind towards his new goal. The desperation in that voice was too great to ignore, more than reminding him of that horrible day so many years ago.

The wind led him around piles of snow that were taller than he ever would be. The dunes hid the voice from his sensitive ears. The wind changed directions many times. He realized it was guiding him through a labyrinth of ice and snow that he never would have been able to navigate alone. Each step took him farther from the path home and brought him closer to some unknown fate. No longer even able to pretend he could hear the helpless appeal, he walked for what seemed like hours, trying to find its cause. He had to trust himself completely to the wind for guidance. He didn't like the sensation.

The gusts finally released him near the bank of a large dune of snow. He looked around and wondered why the wind had brought him there. But when he tried to move away, the wind scolded him like a little child. He thought he heard laughter in it, which served to unnerve him more than anything else had that night. "All right! What do you want now?" His harsh question hung in the air, leaving him feeling disconcerted for talking to the wind.

Clarence kicked at the edge of the drift out of pure frustration. He stopped when his boot hit something with a thud. Something that was softer than ice. He immediately began to brush the cold flakes away from whatever lay hidden beneath, and ended up sitting back in surprise at what he'd found. Right before him was a young woman, whose age he could only begin to guess at. She was wearing nothing but a torn up ensemble of rags, with no cloak or coat to warm her freezing body. Her lips were icy blue with exposure, her skin a shade or two lighter. It surprised him that she wasn't dead. But her breath came in small threads of mist, confirming what the weak pulse under his fingers had already told him. She was alive.

Standing in indecision for several heartbeats, he rocked back on his heels, thoughts racing. Should he take her in? What if she was something different from what she appeared to be? What if she was an intruder caught by nature's furry? He mentally traced her outline in the snow, wondering how she'd gotten there in the first place. If he left her, she would die. That much was certain, but could he risk bringing her with him?

Clarence shook his head, stamped cold feet, and tried to drive back the numbness that had crept in. No, he would not leave her. Whatever he was, he wasn't heartless, though he would need to be careful about how he proceeded with this. He would have to tell both Dena and Santa about his find, along with delivering the reports from the break-in to them. Maybe the two incidents were somehow connected. Maybe not. But he would find out, one way or another.

Wrapping her in the excess of his cloak, he shivered as her skin touched his, but not because of cold. It was more from surprise at how warm her skin was, considering the circumstances. She seemed to weigh next to nothing in his arms. He glanced at her pale face, which seemed almost familiar, like from a dream only half remembered. It felt like déjà vu in the most uncomfortable sense of the word. Or, maybe, it was the overwhelming sense that something was going according to some great plan. Somehow, like his decision to walk home, this felt right. Even if he didn't like it.

Starting back the way he'd come, he finally managed to shrug off the unsettling sensation of crossing swords with fate. He filed the observation away for later examination. Right now, there was a task he had to finish, and such thoughts would only distract him from the here and now.

Clarence slowly found his way back to the path through the labyrinth he'd come through. It surprised him that the wind now left him alone. The arctic breeze only blew just enough to help guide him through the maze of snow and ice. The stars shed their light through the ever-increasing holes in the clouds and he found he was glad that spring was well underway.

TWO

ARTIFICIAL LIGHT FILLED the room, shining off pale walls and blinds. The light fell on what little furniture adorned the place. A nightstand stood to the left of the bed, a small table in the far corner, and a chair to the right. Clarence sat there and stared at the covered windows. They were right next to the door where a small cubicle of curtained off space filled the other half of the room. He drummed fingers on one knee and shifted position, staring now at the bed's occupant.

For some reason, he found he was fascinated by the way her chest rose and fell with each breath. Despite that fascination, he looked at her with some suspicion. After all, it wasn't every day that any elf dared go outside without some semblance of descent clothing, let alone a human. Only those who were crazy even attempted such a thing. She must be either crazy or desperate, and desperate people did desperate things. In his experience, only desperate people, like criminals, turned to such extremes.

Perhaps this was the one they all feared would come. Maybe she was some wayward youth who'd run away. Or, perhaps, she was the one who would destroy everything they'd spent centuries building. All things considered, that was the most likely, especially when one took into account the timing of events. It was also possible that she was one who had broken into all those Observer Stations. The person had left nary a trace behind, other than a few tales and shadows to speculate over. Of course, she might just be a criminal running from the law. Or, maybe, she was that phantom who'd been sending them threatening letters since last October.

Those who are hunted also run, his heart tried to say but he silenced it. "Hunted by the authorities, no doubt," he told himself.

Clarence wished he'd been there during the few moments she'd been awake, even though it had only been a short amount of time. He'd had other duties he'd needed to take care of, not that anything had come of those few minutes. Nothing he knew about at any rate. Apparently the girl had been too incoherent to determine anything during that brief interview. Despite that, he had a feeling that today would be his lucky day. This had to be the day when she would finally wake up and know what was going on around her, and be able to confirm his fears.

The girl stirred in her sleep, murmuring something he couldn't catch. No, she didn't look like a criminal, but few did, he reflected. She looked about the age when most youth went against the grain of the law. He guessed seventeen at the oldest. Still, it was better to err on the side of caution than on just looks.

The moment she was awake, he'd question her. After that, he'd contact the proper authorities, despite of what the others might say. He would not let the past repeat itself. They couldn't afford to take any chances, forget that it wasn't his place or responsibility. It didn't matter that Santa and Dena had told him to leave this one alone, that he had no business even being there. Regardless of that fact, he would have his answers, one way or another. He just hoped it would be sooner than anyone else.

Marie began to show signs of waking, with her long

eyelashes beginning to twitch with the effort. She exhaled, and then drew in a deep breath, her nose wrinkling. A faint smile traced across her delicate lips. Maybe she was just coming out of a pleasant dream. *Kudos to her*, Clarence thought sarcastically. He hadn't had a decent night's sleep since he'd brought her in. It had been no picnic to drag her corpse-like body across the frozen ice to the nearest Subway entrance. It was even less fun to cart her to North Pole City and Rachel's care.

Marie's eyes fluttered open but refused to focus, nor did she know if she wanted them to do so. Wisps of dream still clung to them, a scene of peace. It was something she hadn't had in a long time. However, her eyes reacted before she could decide to let them. The image of a man unfolded in front of her, one that looked far too familiar. She let out a fearful sound that could almost be called a scream. Tearing the bedding away from her body, she scrambled for the wall in a blind panic. Her heart pounded, lungs pumping like a billows as adrenaline ran like wild fire in her veins. She felt him reach for her with hands of steel and anticipated the sound of a gun being fired. "No! No! Don't do it! Don't!" Her arms flew out, trying to ward off her attacker, pushing him over with enough force to knock the wind from his lungs.

Clarence lay stunned no more than a few seconds before he picked himself up and lunged at her. He didn't hear the sound of the door opening as he forced her off the bed and pinned her to the ground. He raised one hand, ready to slap her, completely acting without thought. His own heart raced, as he sucked air in and out between his lips in rapid succession.

Marie cringed, expecting a heavy blow that never came. She almost didn't see him hesitate through her faltering gaze. Her mind refused to believe that he'd hesitate. He hadn't before.

Clarence stopped mid-swing. Slowly, he moved his hand back to his side, reason kicking in once more.

Provoked or not, he couldn't hit her. Instead, he stood up and firmly offered her a hand as he looked into frightened hazel-green eyes. A man could drown in those eyes, and he found himself almost succumbing to such effect. He had to shake his head to clear his mind from the numbing sensation.

Marie looked at the offered hand, seeing a venomous snake waiting to strike. She tried to back away, further pinning herself in the corner. Time itself might have stopped in that moment. It seemed to stretch into forever, with the two of them at an impasse, waiting to see who would make the next move.

Clarence took a step towards her, once more offering his hand. "Look, I'm not going to hurt you, all right?"

After another moment of hesitation, she accepted the offering. There was nothing left to lose. But as he gently pulled her to her feet, she took in his strange clothing, his prominent nose and strong features. The movement was more gentle than he thought she deserved.

As Marie looked closer at him, she realized she didn't recognize his face after all. She was half-afraid that her eyes were not telling the truth. It would not have been the first time. She blinked back a few hot tears, not knowing if they came from fear, shame, or pure exhaustion, perhaps from relief. His face was young, almost as young as hers. She had no idea how old he was.

Clarence brushed himself off. His expression was unreadable as he reached for the chair he'd been sitting on and righted it. "I'm glad you're feeling better." *And that you've decided not to attack me again.* "Rachel thinks you'll recover. No frost bite, which is a miracle in of itself," he said gruffly as he sat down. He noted the confused look on her face and found himself looking at her with more curiosity. He added just enough suspicion to cause her discomfort.

Marie warily sat down on the edge of the bed, still unsure of herself. "Where am I?" she asked, her voice shaking. "Who are you? Who's Rachel?" She searched his face, fearing that he might turn into some wild animal that could, and would, tear her apart. As bizarre as the circumstances were, they had to be too good to be true. She couldn't be that lucky.

"Against my better judgment, you're in the Medical Department of North Pole City. I'm Clarence, Head of Operations. Rachel is our Chief Medic," he said with an air of annoyance. "And you are…? " He gave her a pointed look.

Pulling at the bed sheet, she wadded it in her shaking hands to give them something to do. While she did that, she looked for the determination to answer back, encouraging the fire that she felt building within. His tone sparked indignation and she preferred the anger to fear. "Well I like that! You tear me away from my peaceful world where I was happy and all you can say is 'who are you,' and act like I should know you!"

Marie angrily wiped at the tears coursing down her face, tears she was ashamed to show to a complete stranger. "For your information, my name is Marie, and I guess this is yours too." She threw the wadded sheet at him. "I'm sorry to have been a bother to you." She stood. The sudden movement made her long hair fall in cascades over her slim shoulders. As she swung around, her pointed ears announced themselves. It was almost as if they had magically appeared.

"You're an elf," Clarence accused in amazement, finally noticing the shape of her ears. "Where are you from?" Distrust ran through his veins like coursing fire. Chances were she was some kind of rogue elf and not just the criminal he thought her to be. Why, in all this time, hadn't Rachel said something? Why hadn't he noticed before now?

"I'm from nowhere." Marie glared at him for a moment before looking down at hands that shook with checked rage and shame. She turned away, guessing part of his thoughts. *Why should I tell him my past?* She flung her hair forward to hide her ears from view. She crossed slender arms across her chest, like she was trying to hold herself together by pure force of will. *He'd never understand. He's better off not knowing. How can I trust him, especially after what just happened? He--*

"Tearing you away from your happiness my hat," Clarence interrupted her thoughts. "I find you, an elf who has most likely been trying to freeze to death in a suicide attempt, and all you can be is snooty. Not so much as a 'thank you' or anything."

Marie's eyes went wide. "Snooty? And what are you?" She clenched fists more tightly and turned to glare at him. Her legs began to tremble from the pent up emotions. Indecision fought inside as she tried to decide what to do about this whole crazy situation. It was something that was rapidly spinning further and further out of control.

Clarence placed his hands on his hips as he stood, not bothering to mask his suspicions. "Don't you dare take that tone with me, young lady. Do you have any idea who I am?" He glared at her, his mind going a million miles a minute as he tried to process everything that had happened in the last few minutes. No matter how much he added things up in his head, nothing made sense and that angered him even more.

Marie rolled her eyes in exasperation. "Let me guess, you're the head honcho."

"No."

"Then I don't want to talk to you." She turned her back to him again. Out of all the people she'd met, he was turning out to be one of the most self-absorbed, obnoxious people she'd ever had to deal with.

"Fine. If you won't talk to me you'll talk to the Head Elf." Clarence walked towards the door, making more noise than usual. His footsteps practically screamed as he stomped forward. After a moment, he turned to see if she was following. "Are you coming or what?"

"No, she's not." Heels clacked on the tiles as Rachel stepped out from around the curtained cubicle. "At least not until I approve the discharge. You know the rules, Clarence. You wouldn't want a death on your hands for disobeying me, would you?"

Clarence took a large step back as the medic moved further into the room. He watched as her light hair swung around her youthful face, cheeks rosy with health. He straightened up to tower half a foot over her petite frame, giving off the false sense that she was only thirteen or fourteen years old. "I'd think that highly unlikely if she hasn't keeled over by now," he retorted.

Rachel gave him a sharp look as she passed him. "Oh stop being such a child!" She turned her attention to her patient, intent on ignoring the obnoxious elf. "Let me ask you something. Are you insane? There are a few things you have to learn if you're going to live here long. The first is to not risk the wrath of Clarence. And while we're on the subject, what possessed you? Going outside in rags, I mean. You could have frozen to death!"

"I..." Marie felt her anger drain away as she sat back on the bed. Confusion filled the void the anger had left behind. She closed her eyes and wished for everything to just go away. This could not be happening; it had to be a dream, a bad one judging by the way things were going.

Not to be brushed aside, Clarence moved closer. "I'm not a child, Rachel. And you have no right to treat me like one, " he glared at her. "If I were in charge--"

"Well, you're not in charge so deal with it," Rachel snapped back. "I have work to do." She pushed him aside and began to examine her patient, frowning at the new marks. "There are a few more bruises than I recall from before." She looked at Clarence with disapproval. She was more than aware of what had transpired before she'd intervened.

Clarence growled like a sullen kitten, arms folded across his chest. "What did you expect? She attacked me!

I'm sure you saw the whole thing. It wasn't my fault. Besides, she's lucky, lucky that I didn't leave her out there. I could have, you know."

Rachel gave him a sharp look that somehow seemed more intimidating coming from her youthful face than it should have. It caused him to shrink back a step or two. "Don't even go there. That was days ago, done and over with." She put her hands in the air and turned them as if to brush the topic aside.

"Stop it!" Marie put her hands over her ears, trying to block out their arguing, moving away from the doctor's probing hands. "Stop talking about me as if I'm not here! I am here. And just what are you talking about?" She wiped at her eyes, angry that more tears leaked out against her will.

Rachel sighed, disapproval lining her previous expression as she glanced at Clarence. "I tried to tell you but you couldn't leave well enough alone." She turned to her patient with serious eyes. "I'd hoped I wouldn't have to tell you this yet, but it seems I don't have much of a choice." She shot Clarence a look, warning him to wait while she explained. He ground his teeth in frustration.

"It was about four days ago that he found you out on one of the ice fields near here. Your body temperature was low and your pulse almost non-existent, though he swears it couldn't be as low as it was. We were afraid you might not make it through the first hour, let alone the first day. It was touch and go for a while. Not even the Head Elf had much hope that you'd survive. We were all surprised by the end of the day. After all, it was one of the coldest days on record."

Marie sat back at the medic's tone. "Why bother?" Her tone was flippant, but pain reflected in its depths. "I mean, you don't know me. I'm a stranger here." *Why would you care? No one has before. At least not that I can remember.*

Rachel pursed her lips in thought, one hand in the pocket of her lab coat. "Fair question. I have several different answers. One, I'm a healer. Two, there were too many unexplained things about you," she answered. "It was obvious you'd been out there for a while. You should have been dead. That's why the lack of frostbite was a bit of an eye opener, you might say. The clothes you were wearing wouldn't have kept the cold out for more than a minute. And then there was Clarence." She let it drop at that, unwilling to voice the other elf's theory of criminality.

The seriousness in Rachel's tone stunned Marie. "Where are my clothes? What did you do with them?" She looked down at the hospital gown they'd put her in. "I can't go around in just this." *What about Clarence? Why did he even have a say in the matter?*

"Unfortunately we had to get rid of your old clothes," Rachel apologized. "You'll have to make due with the ones I put in that cubicle over there. I thought you might be up today. And since everything checks out, I see no reason to keep you. Just report back in a few days for a follow-up, sooner if you feel woozy or light headed."

"Just like that, huh," Clarence interjected as he glared daggers at the head medic. "Well, it's about time." He turned towards Marie, toes all but tapping with impatience. "Well, what are you waiting for? Hurry up already! It's not like we have until Christmas for you to play around!"

Marie ducked into the cubicle like a frightened rabbit and changed as fast as she could with fumbling fingers. She had to remind herself to try and slow down to make things easier. She took a few extra seconds to try and compose herself before leaving the protective curtains. It was quiet outside, as she emerged in a pair of loose fitting pants and a blouse, definitely not her style. She almost wished for a mirror but changed her mind at the thought of red tear streaks. Instead, she hoped for a sink full of cold water to splash on her face, though she doubted they'd offer one.

Clarence shook his head with impatience as Marie emerged. He grabbed her arm with the firmness of a steel trap. "Come on. The Head Elf's a busy man and doesn't have all day to waste because you want to play around. " He started for the door, dragging her behind him.

"Hey! Let go," Marie exclaimed, pulling away. "I'm not an escaped criminal you know." She rubbed her wrist, wincing at the red mark left on her skin. "You can't treat me like that."

"Aren't you? Can't I," Clarence almost said aloud, but caught himself just in time.

Rachel inserted herself between the two elves, pulling Marie to one side by the arm. "You know what his problem is? He needs a girl who will cross him once in a while, someone with an equal temper. Someone who can teach him a lesson. Then we'd see how big of a hotshot he really is. Don't get me wrong, he's a nice guy when he wants to be."

Marie looked at her like she was crazy. "What do you mean?" *Why are you telling me this? Am I the only sane one here? This isn't any of my business!* Rachel rewarded her with a shrug that said, "you'll see", and then let her go.

Marie didn't get a chance to say good-bye or try to cipher what Rachel's comment meant. Clarence whisked her out of the medical wing before she could draw breath. His hair bobbed with the energy of his strides, as he dragging her behind like a child's toy, practically charging down the hallway. She noticed how much he tried to not look at her. Her attention was so wrapped up in noticing this that she had no time to look around. She thought they might have gone outdoors and up a few flight of steps but wasn't sure. They were inside now, how ever significant that was.

Clarence finally let her go as they entered a large foyer where another elf sat at a desk. Marie stifled a laugh, something that surprised herself and her expression showed it. The petite elf at the desk was trying to keep her long, light brown hair from getting caught in an old fashioned typewriter. She wasn't doing a good job of it either, as the long strands kept getting tangled in the keys

Still upset over Rachel's comments from earlier, Clarence couldn't appreciate Marie's laughter. She obviously thought the whole situation was some kind of joke. It was a thought that did not improve his mood. "Dena," Clarence half barked out of surprise, stopping in his tracks. "Where's Sandra?" He looked around, trying to see if the younger elf was somehow hiding the secretary.

Dena shrugged her shoulders and continued to type, finally getting her hair safely away from the keys. She hadn't missed the look of surprise on Marie's face and wondered at it. She was more than aware of the thoughts running through Clarence's head. All she had to do was look at his drawn face. She mentally shook her head and filed the incident away for later perusal.

"Oh, never mind," Clarence snapped. He wondered if every female in the North Pole had decided on some kind of personal vendetta against him. He resented the mere idea. "Dena, this is Marie, from 'No Where.' Marie, this is Dena, the Head of the Security League and our security chief."

Dena nodded and continued to type, even though the introduction reminded her of freezer burned ice. "So you're new here. I guess that's why I've never seen you before," she absently peered up through silky hair. She was fully aware that this was the girl her colleague had taken in, against his own better judgment. He'd made that quite clear the moment he'd carried her into the building. Despite that opinion, both she and the Head Elf had already decided to make things as non-threatening as possible for their new arrival. They both knew Clarence would more than make up for the lack thereof. "Maybe Clarence will be nice for a change," she commented. "Don't let him bother you, though. He just tries to act like he's more important than he is. "

Dena seemed the friendly type, Marie thought, if not a little ditsy in manner. Her warm tone suggested she could be counted as a friend though. She needed a good friend. "I don't know about the nice bit, but he did give me the impression that he was someone important." Marie moaned to herself. *What's going on here? Why are they all telling me these things about someone I never want to get to know?*

"So, is the Head Elf in? Or should we come back later," Clarence asked through gritted teeth as he nodded at a closed door. All this senseless chatter unnerved him, especially since it was about him. He wasn't sure what the motive behind his female co-workers' idle prattle was. They were all such a nosy bunch and he wished they'd just stop.

"Oh, he's definitely in. Go right ahead. I don't think he'll mind," Dena waved at the door in haphazard fashion as she hunkered back down to the keyboard. It was obvious that she wasn't used to the old typeset as she hen-pecked her way around the keys.

Clarence breathed a sigh of relief, thankful that his coworker wasn't going to press the issue any further. He was at a loss as to why she was acting a lot more absent-minded than usual. "Thanks. Don't be surprised if we're out in a flash." *Especially with the way Marie seems to be*, he thought with half a snort, far from impressed with what'd he'd seen so far.

He motioned for his charge to follow, dispensing with tugging her like a reluctant child. He didn't want to make Dena and her politics of friendship mad. Dena could definitely take him down if she'd wanted to, even though the security chief was smaller than him.

THREE

SANTA'S OFFICE WAS spacious, even with everything it held. Various pieces of Victorian furniture were scattered across the room. A set of French doors opened out from the far wall, letting in rich, life-giving light. That light accented the red highlights in the cherry-wood desk that almost sat in the middle of the room.

Behind the cherry-wood desk sat an elderly gentleman, his long, white beard only leaving Marie to guess at his age. She felt he could have been mistaken for an older version of a handsome gnome, if it weren't for his human features and large belly. He rested his head in one hand, a feather quill pen in the other. To the left of his hand lay an open pot of indigo, which was next to a piece of thick paper, ready for the quill that had not yet touched ink.

The man looked up, having heard the knock on the door and nodded. He recognized Clarence through the crack, knowing what he'd come for. "Come in. Come in. Don't just stand there waiting on ceremony. You'll let all the cold air in." He beckoned both towards some chairs in front of the impressive desk.

Clarence led Marie into the room at the Head Elf's invitation. But once they were inside, he just stood there and stared ahead until Santa cleared his throat, reminding him of his manners. He shot Marie a look as if it were her fault, then turned to his superior. "Santa, allow me to present Marie the Elf. She claims to come from 'No Where.'" He cast a sideways glance at his charge, eyes all but rolling.

Santa, of course, had already seen her while she'd been in the Medical Department. Though, he doubted Clarence knew that. He gave a nod of acknowledgement, dark eyes twinkling with a warm smile. He half fancied Clarence giving a stiff military bow but shook the thought away. It threatened to make him laugh.

"Marie, this is the Head Elf, Santa Claus," Clarence continued with the introductions. He pronounced Santa's name like one would to a small child, using a sarcastic tone that amused the Head Elf.

Marie looked into Santa's deep hazel eyes. "A pleasure to meet you, sir," she said. She feared her emotions might betray her, even though his face was kind. She was sure that the tear streaks already had.

Santa tilted his head a bit as he gestured for her to sit in the Victorian wing chair. He rested the knuckles of one hand on his lower lip for a brief moment, contemplating what his eyes saw and ears heard. "So, you're from No Where. I've never heard of such a place. May I inquire where it is located," he asked, teasing her as curiosity lined his smile-wrinkled face.

She looked past him, keeping her face as neutral as possible. "No Where is just that, nowhere. It's no place, no time. I don't claim to come from anywhere." She didn't appreciate his teasing tone. At least he didn't seem to have the nasty tendency of trying to provoke her like Clarence did. And he hadn't given her unwanted information about the rather rude Head of Operations either.

Mr. Claus left his chair and started to pace the room, leaving his antique pipe on the desk. He didn't even know why he kept it. He never smoked, but it was part of his heritage, not to mention that many young people seemed to picture him with one in hand. "Hmm. Most interesting. An elf from nowhere is always a matter of interest to me. There are usually so many things behind that kind of reasoning."

Marie followed his progress around the room with her eyes, not daring to move from her seat. "I would appreciate it if you didn't try to reason me out, sir. There are some things that are best left alone." *Like my past. I don't need anyone digging that up and hurting me again. At least what I can remember of it.* Her eyes narrowed just a little, forcing her mouth to droop into a slight scowl.

Clarence eyed his superior's face. He realized the Head Elf might not be taking the situation with the seriousness it required. What was Santa doing, playing games? He held that thought in check. Santa knew what he was doing. He recrossed his arms, making sure he stood to one side of Marie, where he could keep a close eye on her every move.

"All right," the elderly elf conceded as he paused, "but that still leaves me with a question. What am I going to do with you? I can't just throw you out. In a manner of speaking, of course. That would be unthinkable. It would be like throwing you back to the wolves," he mused, knuckles on chin once more. "There must be something you can do here." He continued his turn around the room.

After a moment's meditation, Santa gave a quick nod, like he'd just agreed to some silent advice. "I could let you work here as my secretary's personal assistant, on a probationary term of course. What do you say to that, Clarence?" He gave a small wink at his Head of Operations, though it could have been mistaken for a twitch.

Clarence shifted his feet, a scowl stretching across his face. He knew he'd never get out of having to play the baby-sitter to this unknown elf. It didn't help that there was something about this girl that made his skin crawl. Why Santa didn't feel it, he didn't know. He couldn't quite put his finger on it either, but his earlier misgivings would not let matters lie. She shouldn't be anywhere near any of the records Sandra was given charge over.

"I see," Santa said, eyeing the elf. "I guess it's a new idea for you too. Well, I'll have to think about it a bit more, I suppose. You never can be too careful." He turned back to face Marie. "Still, there is something about you, Marie, that intrigues me. I just can't put my finger on it."

Clarence blinked. "What did you say, sir?" He mentally kicked himself for letting his thoughts drift away from the conversation at hand.

Santa raised a brow at the distracted tone from his right-hand elf. "I said I can't figure out why I feel that my idea was a good one. It's obvious you weren't paying attention," he chided.

Clarence frowned. "That's not what you said. I'm sure I heard you say something else."

Santa shrugged. "Does it matter? If you know I said something different, then you must have heard me the first time. That being the case, there is no need for me to repeat what I said."

Clarence wanted to shake him. He wanted to yell and scream, "Yes, it does matter!" He couldn't take it anymore. The entire day had been one jumble of consternation and bad karma. *I don't know what Santa's up to but there's something fishy going on here.* He clenched and unclenched his fist, forcing himself to relax. Santa knew what he was doing. He kept repeating that to himself. Just what Santa was doing was beyond him.

He left Marie's side and paced, trying to think of a sure-proof way to get her out of his hair. Maybe if he presented an idea that was so ludicrous he might get out of playing watchdog to some newcomer with no known past history. After all, it was possible that she was the criminal she denied to be. Or was that what he wanted? He didn't know. He hadn't been sure about anything since he'd first laid eyes on her.

"Why don't you just make her your Emergency Replacement instead of Sandra's assistant?" Clarence blurted. His words tumbled out before he could even think about the implications. "You've always wanted to have someone just in case of an emergency." His eyes sparkled with vexation, knowing he was being impertinent but not caring. He was sure Santa would never consider his suggestion with any seriousness.

Santa smoothed his beard. He measured the risks and the information his wizened eyes gave him. He included the intentions of his Head of Operations. He rubbed his chin, looked to one side, and nodded. "That's not a bad idea. It's nice to have someone. Just in case." He strode back to the desk and picked up a quill. "It does sound reasonable. All right, why don't we do just that? It will give her full access to all Leagues and privileges due to someone up that high. She'll pretty much be equal with you, Clarence." He gave his elf a knowing glance, eyes twinkling as he wrote down Marie's name and new position. The elf had played right into his hands, not that it had been all that hard to persuade him. They had both known the position was necessary and had discussed it at great lengths recently.

Clarence stared back, jaw somewhat agape. He'd only said it to vent his frustration, a mere joke; a joke that seemed to have been taken far too seriously. "But Santa! You can't think I was serious!"

The Head Elf held up a finger. "No ifs, ands, or buts about it. I think it's a great idea. Truth be told, it's possibly the best you've ever had." Santa gave him a stern look that didn't reach his jovial tone. "I wonder why I didn't think of it myself." *Someone needs to keep tabs on you too.* He rubbed his chin again. It would hit two birds with one stone, as there was always the possibility that he'd at least temporarily be unable to fulfill his duties as the Head Elf. They all hoped that would never happen, even though there were precedents for it.

"But you can't be serious," Clarence tried again. "I mean..." He dropped his hands in exasperation and defeat, knowing that once Santa made a decision, it was rarely ever repealed.

Santa stared into the elf's eyes. "No, Clarence. You can be assured that I am quite serious about this. I know what you're likely thinking, but you're the one who got yourself into this mess. For as old as you are, even you still have a lot to learn."

Marie stood up, breaking the tension between the two men. A pained smile spread across her face, brows drawn together in worry. "Thank you. I don't know what I'd have done if you'd turned me out. I would have had no where to go." Inside she felt sick. *What am I doing? What if he finds me here? I don't want to get hurt again, and I can't let him hurt anyone else either. I'm sure no matter where I go, he will find me again and finish what he started.*

"Then it's all settled, " Santa declared. He placed an official looking stamp at the bottom of the document he'd been drafting. A loud knock sounded on the door as he lifted the seal and a blonde-haired elf peered around the doorjamb. Santa turned his attention to her, folding the document with one hand. "Yes? What is it, Sandra?"

"Santa, we've got a problem. It's Miles in Wrapping." Sandra glanced at Marie with some curiosity. She'd missed meeting her due to an errand that couldn't be put off.

The Head Elf sighed. "I'll be right there." He gave one last look around the office, shook his head, and made to follow the secretary out the door as he slipped the paper to Clarence. He stopped long enough to pat Marie on the shoulder. "This place isn't perfect but it's the best we have to offer." He turned, "Clarence, I want you to take her by Dena's for an ID card. You're also in charge of taking her for a run in the sleigh; sometime in the next few weeks would be good. Make sure you train her in all she needs to know and make sure you teach her the correct signals for lift-off and landing. Give her a tour of the city while you're at it." He looked over the rims of his glasses, pausing just for a moment as he contemplated his stubborn friend. "And Clarence, be nice."

"I'd rather let Dena do that, the tour I mean. They've already formed a bond." Clarence glanced sideways at Marie. She didn't seem to notice.

"That's fine," Santa agreed. "But you need to take care of all the rest. After all, she's your responsibility now."

Clarence nodded with gritted teeth. *You had to remind me.* He turned to Marie, who was just standing there like some kind of statue. "This way. We'll visit Dena first. Don't touch anything. I'm warning you in advance, I'm not in a good mood."

FOUR

MARIE FOLLOWED CLARENCE down the hallway, keeping an arm's length from him. She harbored bruises from their previous jaunt down the hallway and didn't feel like adding more. She was just glad he'd let her wash the tear streaks off her face before heading off to find Dena once more. It didn't matter since the security chief had already seen them, but it did make her feel better about everything.

"So..." She let her voice trail off as they walked. "Is Dena Santa's secretary too?" She'd noticed that the elf in question had not been outside Santa's office when they'd left.

Clarence didn't even check his stride. "Of course not. Don't you know anything?"

Marie looked at his back and grit her teeth. "I guess not. I'll try to be more observant next time so that I'll know everything in advance." *That, or learn how to read minds.*

The Head of Operations didn't say anything. Instead, he quickened his pace, forcing her to jog to keep up. His legs were definitely longer than hers. It was something he took full advantage of, if only to express his own feelings on the situation.

Marie was out of breath by the time they'd reached their destination but tried to quiet her breathing as much as possible. Clarence was breathing without difficulty. Did he ever sweat? She tried to take a moment to gather herself back together but couldn't help but stare at the change in scenery.

A bright green and pink desk sat in a corner of the open office area. A purple chair stood behind it. In front of the odd furniture sat three comfortable looking yellow chairs. A hallway led off to a bank of smaller rooms. Marie blinked a few times at this unexpected sight. Clarence had to pull her arm to get her into the first chair. He took the third seat over and crossed his arms in a huff, making sure to maintain as much distance between them as possible.

Noticing their arrival from inside her private office, Dena entered the open office. She noted the seating arrangement, but chose to ignore it for the moment as she smiled. "Hello again. What can I do for you?"

Clarence slid the paper Santa had given him towards the younger looking elf. "Marie needs her file put in the computer and to get her ID card," he said, sounding like he had something stuck in his throat.

Dena nodded. "Let me boot up this old thing. It'll only take a second." She walked around the desk and tapped in the glass looking top.

Marie cast a puzzled look at Clarence. "What's she doing?"

Clarence scowled back. "She's making a file. What does it look like?" He leaned further away in his chair. "Just stay in your seat and don't come any closer to me."

Marie bit her lip but slid back in her chair. For lack of any better place to stare, she focused on Dena's forehead, waiting for the inevitable.

Dena finally looked up and pushed a stray strand of hair out of the way. She'd put most of her hair up into a ponytail, but the one bit had somehow escaped. "Well then, let's get started." With that, she started to fire off questions, recording the responses on her desktop.

Some questions were more personal than others. Some were more mundane, reminding Marie of a personality profile quiz. She answered with what truth she dared. It surprised her how efficient and professional this funny elf had become.

Many questions were left unanswered, much to Clarence's annoyance, but not Dena's. "Trust has to be gained on both sides," Santa had told her and she agreed. They would have to tread with care around this one. There were things here that Clarence hadn't been told yet, things Santa thought best not to tell him. Dena just wondered how some of those things had happened, like the scar on Marie's back. Rachel said it had come from a gunshot wound. And then there was the haunted look she kept seeing in her eyes. Clarence might choose to ignore it, but she wouldn't.

The security chief mentally noted Marie's reactions to every question. She also noted every reaction towards Clarence and herself. She already knew her colleague didn't share any desire to become more than acquainted with their new team member. She couldn't help but feel a small amount of pity for her. It definitely wasn't an enviable position to be in.

Dena agreed with Santa's sentiments about her, though. Marie seemed so lost, so afraid. There was definitely something about her that they couldn't quite put a finger on. There had to be something they could do to help her, and to figure out what was going on. She already knew Clarence's view on the matter, though she didn't agree with him. The word criminal did not seem to fit in this situation. More like fugitive.

After a while, Dena left off with the questions and gave Marie time to ask any of her own. She didn't have many to answer and noted that might have been because of Clarence's presence. She glanced in his general direction, and then nodded to herself. "Did I overhear Santa asking you to give Marie a tour of the city once we were done here?" She gave him a piercing glance. Technically speaking, she hadn't been spying on them, even if she had listened to the entire exchange through the door.

"Actually, Santa wanted you to," Clarence said, his eyes narrowed. "Why?"

"No reason," Dena smiled sweetly. "I'll take over from here then, if you don't mind. You can leave her with me. Don't worry, I'll make sure she finds her way around."

Marie switched her gaze from one elf to the other, wondering what was going on between them. The tension in the air was almost tangible, though Dena seemed to be the one with the upper hand.

Clarence and Dena locked eyes for a brief moment before he broke away with a shrug. "It doesn't matter to me. You do what you want anyway."

"True," she half smirked. "I do have that privilege. I'm so glad you don't mind." Her smile spread across her face.

Clarence sighed, a disgusted look on his face. "Have fun, Dena. And watch your back. You never know what she might do," he quipped as he started to leave.

"Clarence!" Dena started after him but stopped, knowing that going after him was pointless. "That was uncalled for. You come back here and apologize." He ignored her calls, continuing down the corridor without so much as a backward glance.

Dena tapped a finger on her cheek as she sighed. A frown creased her face when she turned around. "Ignore him. He's just being a boy." *I can't believe he's taking this so far. Stupid, stupid boy.*

"I've known a lot of boys in my life," Marie commented, " and that's not what I'd call typical behavior. He doesn't like me but I don't know why."

Dena moved over to her new charge, trying to lighten the mood. "Don't worry about it. Come on. I hear the kitchen's serving up hot chili today. Don't give Clarence a second thought. The way he goes on, you'd think he'd learned everything before he was two years old." She rolled her eyes.

Marie followed her through an archway, feeling more confused than ever. "Maybe you could take me on that tour Santa talked about. Before the chili, I mean. I don't think I could handle it right now. I've kind of lost my appetite."

"I know what you mean. Spiders have the same effect on me," Dena laughed.

"Spiders?" Marie raised her brows and tried to memorize the hallway they walked down. She had no idea what spiders had to do with the situation, unless she meant Clarence was one, which almost made sense. Almost.

"Yes, spiders." Dena confirmed. "Clarence doesn't scare me and you shouldn't let him scare you either. The only real thing that scares me is a spider. They make me lose my appetite every time, especially if they bungee off the ceiling."

"Right." Marie blinked in confusion. "About that tour?"

"Oh, right." Dena laughed. "Follow me. We'll start here at the Main Rotunda." She moved towards one of the many arched doorways spaced around the large room they'd entered. "It might take you a while to get used to all the corridors in this building but you'll get the hang of it. You'll be working in here a lot with your duties. Clarence will see to that. The city itself is less complex."

"City?" Marie's eyes went wide. "You mean there's more than just this building? I thought the North Pole was all under one roof." She tried to remember her trip from the Medical Department but found she only remembered looking at Clarence's broad back.

"Common misconception." Dena stopped and turned to look at Marie. "We house thousands of elves and dozens of different departments. You didn't think we could put it all under one roof did you? Why, this place would have to be as big as the Empire State Building to do that. And we don't keep everything here in North Pole

City either. There are other cities around the world, including in the South Pole."

Marie pressed a hand to her forehead, taking a step back. "The South Pole?" She shook her head. Something about even hearing that region named made her headache even worse. "Why doesn't the rest of the world know about you then? I mean… wouldn't it be kind of obvious with several cities full of elves?"

Dena shook her head with a smile. "You'd think that, but no. North Pole City and South Pole City are carefully hidden, along with our various junction points and safe houses. North Pole City was built into a giant, stationary iceberg, which you won't find on any maps. We're a long ways from the surface here. The reason we don't get cold is it's like a giant igloo. And we have some really advanced heating systems that don't melt the ice dome. Not to mention the fact that all our energy is recycled."

"Dome?" Marie asked. From her vantage, the ceiling loomed above them. To think there was something even higher up was more than she wanted to contemplate.

Dena smiled. "Yes, dome. It's made out of ice but is maintained by special technology we developed here in the City. Think of it like a giant snow globe covered over with a thick layer of ice. Add to that an access hole, or tunnels that lead to the surface, and you should get the picture. It's all camouflaged to look like the rest of the tundra from above."

Marie let out her breath, trying to take this idea in stride. "To think all this exists without anyone the wiser. I guess you kind of encourage adults to believe this place isn't real. You don't get many outsiders up here do you?"

Dena started walking towards the nearest archway. "There have been a few that had no business being here who did manage to get in. That's part of the reason for a Security League, but it doesn't happen often. There are too many rumors and other misinformation planted to keep them off our tracks. Then, of course, there are always backup plans in case something like that should happen.

"We did have an intruder a couple years back." She looked thoughtfully at the door in front of her before turning back to her guest. "It caused quite a stir. We eventually caught the man but it took a while to bring things back to normal."

"You mean people have broken in here before?" Marie tried to picture that happening but couldn't. Who would come out to an old iceberg anyway?

"Yes," Dena said. "It's not something we tell people, if you know what I mean. But we can talk about that later. Right now, it's time to show you North Pole City as it really is."

They stepped up to a set of double doors made with intricately designed glass. Marie looked at the ornate doorknobs so she wouldn't spoil the view before they were opened. Dena smiled and pushed the doors open. "Welcome to North Pole City."

FIVE

LATE MORNING LIGHT shown down through glittering stalactites suspended from the ice dome. The dome was over a mile high and at least a dozen miles in diameter. The light shown on a multitude of buildings, every building with its own design. Some seemed to be spun from sugar. Other buildings were sturdier looking. Those buildings were made of either wood, brick, or some other material Marie couldn't identify. Dena took her to see them all.

One part of the city held the toy factories. Unlike in normal human suburbia, no clouds of smoke or smog filled the air. The streets and sidewalks were swept clean. Some of the streets had rails laid on them, and had little platforms every couple hundred yards. Marie wondered at this but made no comment. Going inside the buildings was more fascinating.

Elves were busy at work inside the toy factories, each doing a different task. Some were painting dolls; others were putting together various toys. Each department had a different supervisor, and a regular shift of workers. Marie was surprised by how much it reminded her of human factories, only more efficient and cleaner. And the workers looked a lot happier, with some even singing and dancing as they worked.

"As part of your duties, you will make rounds of inspection with Clarence," Dena noted as they walked down one section. "Santa likes him to keep an eye on all operations, even with the supervisors keeping tabs." She gestured towards one supervisor who was walking through his designated area with a clipboard.

"You mean I have to work with him? On a daily basis?" Marie's face filled with horror.

"Yes," Dena confirmed. "It's part of your duties now. You're equal in rank with him and share some of the same responsibilities. But don't let him push you around just because he's big and macho and 'has more experience'."

Marie resisted the urge to bite her lip. "That's a little easier said than done. I'm more of a quiet, non-fighting kind of girl. I've always had a problem standing up for myself or voicing my opinions."

Dena looked at her. Marie's statement wasn't consistent with her own observations. "You don't seem to have any trouble talking with me. And you didn't seem to have any problems standing up to Clarence in Med. Dept. Word does get around," she added, seeing the look in Marie's eye.

"It's different around you," Marie countered. "You don't make me feel like an outsider." *And you don't treat me like a criminal.*

Dena waved a hand. "I was voted the 'most friendly elf' as a child, and the most ditsy. I personally find it easier to get along with people if I treat them the way I want to be treated. It's nothing big."

"It is to me." Marie smiled in appreciation. "Only you and Santa have treated me like a normal person so far. I'm just a patient to Rachel. And to Clarence I'm just a pebble in his shoe."

"That's such a cliché comment," Dena said, rolling her eyes as she directed her to the next building, the Candy

Factory. "I wonder what Clarence would say to that." She smiled at the idea.

"Some snide comment no doubt," Marie muttered under her breath.

Dena stopped in the middle of a walkway and raised a brow at her new friend. "You don't like him do you? Mind if I share a bit of advice? Don't read too much into what Clarence says or does. It doesn't matter what he thinks. All that matters is what you think. You have to be the strong one, extend the hand of friendship. He won't, not until you've earned his trust, on his terms."

Marie threw her hands up in frustration. "And what will that take? Excuse me for being blunt, but I don't think that's likely to happen any time soon. His opinion of me was set the moment I woke up, and probably even before that. I can't help it if I somehow managed to scare him. He scared the living daylights out of me too. That doesn't give him the right to try and put me down."

Dena sensed they'd hit a sore topic. "I think we should talk about something else," she maneuvered. "For example here at the Candy Factory we turn out thousands of pounds of sugary confections a month. Those that we don't make here are ordered from different companies all over the world. We often trade out as well."

Marie let her attention travel to the elves working at various stations, making all kinds of delicious treats. She recognized some of the confections, but there were others she did not. "With all this candy you make, why bother getting any from other companies? Why trade out?"

Dena snitched a chocolate from one of the conveyer belts and popped it between her lips. "We have to get our supplies from somewhere. We grow or make what we can and the rest we get through trade or we buy it. That includes items for the other departments. Not all of our elves work in workshops. Some have regular working jobs in the big cities. They're the ones who've learned to use their 'magic', if you will. They can use it to make themselves look older, or other useful stuff like disguising their features. Elves, by nature, are almost eternally young, you know.

"We also have several corporations that we own, some famous ones for that matter. That's partly how we're able to interact with humans without suspicion. There are also some humans who work with us. You may not have noticed but not all the workers here in the city are elves." She waved to a worker who waved back.

"We use a system of Observers, and something like study abroad. Some elves share physical similarities with normal humans. With that person's consent, they trade places. The elf takes on the life of the human and vice a versa. It's a great way to get elves out in the 'real' world."

Marie glanced down at one of the gratings covering a drain. "But doesn't that put you in some kind of jeopardy with security?" *That makes it way too easy. If he'd known about this, he wouldn't have had to go through all that trouble with me.*

Dena shook her head. "Not really. Each participant is carefully screened before any such arrangement is made. They're generally children anyway. Children, as you know, have fantastic imaginations and usually can keep this kind of thing secret. The elf taking their place is carefully instructed on their behavior and habits."

"I guess that makes sense," Marie mused as she ran a finger over a somewhat sugary counter top. "Can we go to a different building now? I feel kind of sticky with all this sugar in the air."

"Sure," Dena consented. "We can visit the library. It's a nice little structure with a lot of books." She directed her in the appropriate direction. Marie laughed a bit at that comment. Of course a library had books!

The library held more books than Marie thought possible. "They're from all over the world," Dena informed, watching Marie's reaction. "I find it beneficial to come here a lot on my off time. I learn all kinds of interesting things here, and a lot that helps with my job."

Marie traced a finger over a bookshelf and held it up for inspection. It was clean. "There's no dust," she looked up in surprise.

"The librarian likes to keep things in tiptop shape," Dena smiled. "You won't find a speck of dust anywhere, not even in the older archives. We should move along though. There are other places to look at before the day is over."

Dena led her to the more urban parts of the city, showing her the apartments and other housing for the elves. Marie was surprised to find them all similar to the first place she remembered ever calling home. She felt a momentary bout of homesickness but pushed it aside. It was easy to remember why she'd never gone back as she shook her head with a quick jerk. No, she would not look back on that. That didn't matter now. Only surviving mattered.

Dena, unsure of why Marie had stopped, gave her a questioning look. "Something wrong?"

Marie shook her head. "Nothing's wrong. I just had a chill. That's all." She wasn't sure if Dena believed her but was glad when she didn't try to push for a better answer. Instead, they talked about the population of North Pole City, its government, and its laws.

During their conversation, Dena showed Marie her own apartment, letting her get an idea of the dimensions. "You'll be living in the Main Office Complex though," Dena warned, "on the floor just above Santa's office. Clarence's room is just down the hall, along with Santa's."

"So they can keep an eye on me," Marie interjected. "I understand. I'm the unknown quotient here. Santa can't trust me. Clarence said so himself."

"What?" Dena stared at her. "Clarence doesn't know what he's talking about. Santa just likes to have his upper personnel close at hand. It has nothing to do with trust. I'd be living up there too if I didn't insist on having things my own way."

Marie didn't make any comment. Instead, she turned her attention back to the buildings they were now passing. One of them was clearly marked as the Post Office. She turned that way, curious to see inside.

"That," Dena said, "is the Post, as most of us call it. A good majority of the letters ever mailed to the North Pole, or Santa, eventually find their way here. Of course, it depends on how cooperative the different mail systems around the world are. Some are a little more stubborn about letting us into their dead letter room than others. And there are a few businessmen in other areas that take on the challenge of writing on Santa's behalf."

"Oh," Marie blinked. She glanced into the different rooms. She was about to head to the next building but Dena motioned her in the other direction. She led her to one of the many platforms Marie had noticed earlier. A set of tracks ran alongside the raised stage. They were not like any railway tracks she'd ever seen. "What are these for," she finally asked.

"You'll see," Dena's eyes twinkled. "It gets sore walking everywhere. It's not possible to get to every point you needed to if you just walked, at least not on time. That's why these were installed. It's also an easier way to see the town."

An old-fashioned trolley came jauntily down the track towards them. "The trolley won't stop but it will slow down," Dena explained. "When it comes next to the platform, just start walking alongside it and grab onto one of the poles. The trick is to hop aboard before you run out of platform to walk on. If you don't, you'll get a nasty jolt as you step down a few feet. Trust me, it's happened before."

"I can't do that!" Marie's eyes went wide with panic as she thought about the potential of even that short of a drop. It was an even less appealing thought to possibly be dragged behind the car. The sensation didn't settle well, causing a cold sweat to break out on her forehead.

Dena placed a hand on her shoulder. "Look, it's slowing down." She directed Marie to the top half of the platform. "Hold out your hand and, as soon as a pole comes by, somewhere in the middle is best, grab it and start walking with the car. A few feet before you hit the end of the platform, just step into the car. It's the same height so there's no need to be afraid." She guided Marie's right hand out towards the incoming trolley. It started to pass, slowing down even more once the driver realized the situation. "I'm right behind you," Dena assured as she let go of Marie's arm. "There's a pole."

Marie hesitated too long and missed the first one. She swallowed as another pole started to pass by but reached out and grabbed it, feeling like her body had been pulled out from under her.

"Walk with it," Dena reminded. She was already on the trolley. Marie started to walk with the car, trying to pace herself with it and her knocking knees. "Swing into the car," Dena encouraged.

Marie tried to comply and managed to make it on before the platform ended under her feet. She hugged the pole like a lifeline as the trolley began to pick up speed.

Dena gave her a moment to regain her composer before drawing her onto a seat. "There now, that wasn't too bad was it?" She smiled. "I don't think even Clarence did that well his first time." She gave her charge a comforting squeeze. "It'll come easier with practice," she assured her.

Marie shook inside. The sensation in the pit of her stomach felt too much like something she'd experienced in the past. She closed her eyes and let a shudder wash over her.

"You okay?" Dena glanced at her with concern. "You look kind of pale."

Marie nodded and pulled her hair back from her face. "It's nothing. I'm fine."

"You sure?" Dena continued to look at her. "We can go see Rachel to be sure."

"No. It's nothing," Marie reaffirmed. "I really just don't like heights. Any heights. That's all."

Dena nodded. "Takes me back to the spider issue. I understand. How about I just show you to your apartment?"

Marie nodded. "I'd like that. Sorry to ruin the tour. I did enjoy myself." She hugged her knees to her chest and tried not to cry.

SIX

SANTA LEANED ON the balcony railing, watching the comings and goings of his elves in the streets down below. It reminded him of a well-organized ant colony, purpose in everything. The main difference was that his elves were not mindless insects bent on a single task. They were a group of individuals working together towards the same goal.

Everything seemed so simple here, simple and almost innocent. Experience had taught him that these elves were not as innocent as the general public believed. They knew what happened all around the world, the good and the bad. It surprised him that none of it had a negative effect on them, or at least most of them. He wasn't sure about their newest member yet. Marie was unlike any elf he knew.

The Head Elf sensed a hidden something inside her, part of it pain, part of it fear. His intuition was usually good. He just couldn't help but feel that Marie's coming would present them all with a trial unlike any they had faced before. He couldn't tell why, but somehow knew, there was something he needed to find out about her, for her safety and that of his other elves.

Santa returned to his desk. It was no use to stare out

the window. He couldn't see either Marie or Dena from there anyway, but that didn't matter. Dena would come and tell him everything soon enough, from every word that was spoken, to every action and reaction. Clarence had informed him that Dena had taken charge of their new friend, at least for the day. He was probably off somewhere, scowling at anyone who crossed his path.

Clarence also held a lot of pain inside. Santa had heard stories about his younger days. One story, in particular, came to mind. He'd accepted a dare to go outside for an extended period of time without a coat. Like most youngsters, he'd accepted the dare but had regretted it later. The cold had done more than freeze his body. His 'friends' had left him there. Alone.

Santa could only imagine what the experience had done to him. Sandra had mentioned that he was angrier now. The two had been close up until that incident. It was surprising. Especially since she'd been the only one who'd stayed behind when all his so-called 'friends' had run off and left him. She was also the only one to visit him in Med. Dept. while he'd recovered from the exposure.

I wonder if the other Santa had just as much trouble with him as I do. He frowned, furrowing brows in thought. *I wonder if he ever came across anyone like Marie.* The only way he would find out would be to read the other man's journal. It was a book kept in the special collections part of the library. He didn't know if he wanted to walk over there or not, though. He could send for it, but didn't feel the need as he shrugged tired shoulders. There was still plenty of time. It was only April, after all. He just had to be patient with Marie, and himself. And hope he could figure this whole thing out before November. If not, there was always the journal.

CLARENCE SULKED. Why wouldn't Santa listen to him? He wanted to just shout his frustrations into the sky but didn't think it would help the situation. It might help him deal with his own feelings, though he doubted it. How could Santa have done this to him? He paced his bedroom and knocked a book to the floor. Was he just being stubborn? What had Santa said? He tried to recall the exact he'd used, running back through the conversation.

"I need you to help Marie settle in. This is a new experience for her and she will need a pillar of strength to rely on."

"A pillar of strength? Ha. You saw how she treated me. She's trouble, I'm telling you."

Santa had sighed. He was getting too old for this. "Clarence, she is alone and afraid, with no one to rely on. No friends. No family. And there are things that we just don't yet know about her that we will need to know. We have to gain her trust if we're to help her."

Then, of course, there was Clarence's scathing reply to that. "I don't trust her, and why you and everyone else does is beyond me. Can't you see it? She's a danger signal on high alert! How could you do this to me?"

Santa understood. He always did, but this time it grated on his nerves. "Clarence," and he could see him shaking his head again, "You must learn to trust at least some people."

"I trust you," he'd replied with a scowl.

"Then trust my judgment."

That was it, the end of the entire frustrating conversation. Clarence made up his mind that he would not rest until the truth was found out, even if it meant he had to force it out of her. But he would not be her friend. Santa was wasting his time in that department. He would teach her what the Head Elf wanted him to, but nothing more. He'd even put up with having to do rounds with her, but that was where he drew the line. Nothing else could induce him to even think about liking her.

Clarence turned off his lamp and slipped into bed, resentment right beside him. It smoldered like hot coals from a fire left to its own devices, continuing to burn long after his eyes were closed and he'd fallen asleep.

It was dark as he ran down the hallways of the Main Office Complex, searching, hoping that what his heart and mind whispered wasn't true. There was no way it could be true. It had to be the worst lie imaginable, but it still sang through his veins. It felt like hot fear burning in a blazing inferno of mixed up emotions.

The radio at his side blared static, jumbled words that were unintelligible. Only the occasional call for haste filtered through. But, no matter how hard he tried to run, to climb down the many stairs, it felt like he was moving through molasses. It felt like he was moving slower and slower the closer he got to the ground floor. It looked like a war zone, with debris strewn all over. It was as if the place had been abandoned because of some kind of attack.

In one hand, he gripped the note he'd found on Santa's desk. The note explained where his friend had gone; even knowing that doing so might spell the end of his life. Why had Santa been so self-sacrificing? Why hadn't he asked for help? Clarence tried to run faster, trying to understand what had gone through the Head Elf's head. He hoped to arrive there before the unthinkable happened. He raced for the doors facing the Green and flung them open, bursting out into the light.

Clarence sat up, chest heaving; sweat pouring off his shivering body as he stared into space. After a moment, he shuddered and closed his eyes, the images still burning behind shut lids. Why was he dreaming about that now? How had those memories been shaken loose?

With a groan, he turned over and looked at the clock, scowling at the numbers. The night was way too young for this. But, with those imagines in his mind, there was no way he would be able to get back to sleep any time soon. It was going to be a long night.

Marie propped her head up with an elbow as she tried to focus on the white board where Clarence was writing down different instructions. She was supposed to be copying them down. Her pencil slipped out of her right hand, falling onto the desk where she sat. She jerked her head up and tried to focus on Clarence's words. She began to nod again, eyes staring ahead without seeing anything, eyelids drooping. She tilted her head towards the left, as if trying to see past him at the equations noted down. Her mouth drooped and her head slipped off of her other hand. She cried out as her head hit the desk.

Clarence turned around, slamming a hand down on his lectern. "Are you awake over there?" He glared, squeezing the marker in one hand until the cap popped off. "You need to pay attention!" He strode over to her desk. "Do you understand, or have you even been listening?"

Marie mumbled an apology and picked up her pencil. "Can't we take a break? We've been at this for hours, and my brain can only handle so much." She rubbed her eyes and stared back.

"If Santa wants you to learn this, then you will learn it," Clarence explained with impatience. "And I will make sure that you do. No matter how many times I have to drill these concepts into your thick skull."

Marie clenched her teeth, balling hands into fists under the desk so he couldn't see them. "I don't recall him saying I had to learn everything within the first week," she retorted.

Clarence put his hands behind his back, feet apart in what he liked to think was military fashion. "His exact words were as follows: 'Sometime in the next few weeks, make sure you train her in all she needs to know. Teach her the correct signals for lift-off and landing.' I intend to do that in half the time. Aside from which, we're in the second week since you first arrived. So no slacking!"

Marie's eyes widened at his little speech. *Is he for real?* "It's almost eight o'clock," she said, reminding him they'd been at this for at least six hours without a decent break. "Can't the rest wait until tomorrow? I don't think I can keep my eyes open much longer, and my brain is rebelling."

Clarence scowled, but looked at his watch. "Fine. But I want to see you here tomorrow morning at six sharp. No excuses." If he couldn't sleep, neither would she.

Marie's jaw almost dropped. "Are you serious?" She didn't know how much more of this she could take. His idea of education would drive her to insanity in record time, something she definitely hoped to avoid. She had enough problems without adding that to the list.

"Yes, I'm serious. Unless you have some other previous engagement, or a life or death situation scheduled. If not, I expect to see you here bright and early and ready to learn." Clarence picked up the marker lid and put it where it belonged, using enough force to make it snap.

"Actually, I do," Marie retorted. "I'm supposed to see Rachel at eight. I don't think she'd like to be kept waiting."

The Head of Operations slammed the marker onto the chalkboard railing. "I will see you at six a.m., and then I will let you go see Rachel. But I expect you back here as soon as you're finished. Failure to show up will be reported to the Head Elf as insubordination."

"Fine!" She picked up her notebook and pushed the pencil through the wire binding. She used enough force to send some of the loops into disarray. She stalked out the door and into the hallway, heading to her room. "Slave driver," she muttered.

Clarence was tempted to call her back to apologize, but he still had a lot of things that needed taking care of. At least she was as miserable as he was, which made him feel a tiny bit happier about the whole situation. Santa wouldn't approve, but it was a small satisfaction that he didn't need to know about.

MARIE WANDERED the halls. Sighing, she closed her eyes and breathed in deeply. She walked out into the night, leaving the Main Rotunda behind her, exchanging it for the large grassy field that comprised the Green. It was filled with so many walkways, perfect for someone in her frame of mind. She headed towards the library, wondering if there might be something there to read that wouldn't put her to sleep. With her luck, Clarence probably controlled access to that too. But when she went in, the building seemed quiet and inviting.

Marie found an empty room that was out of the way of most of the traffic inside. It had several tables with low padded chairs and comfortable decor. Several shelves lined the walls, filled with older volumes. She took down a dark blue one with gold filigree covering. The title was so worn she couldn't read it. It felt heavier than it should, like it contained some infinite wisdom. Either that, or she was loosing it, all thanks to Clarence.

Slowly turning the pages, she felt the difference in the paper's thickness. Some pages were thicker than others, almost as if every page had been hand pressed. As she turned back a few pages, she noticed they were covered in a strong, masculine script. She wasn't sure if she really should be reading this or not. It seemed a bit intrusive. After all, she was sure this had once been someone's journal. But her eyes were already absorbed in the history before she could stop herself.

January 10, 1967

I'm still trying to wrap my head around all this. How on earth did I become the newest Santa? It's unreal, and my dear wife, Elena, is having a hard time coming to terms with it, even though she's being more than supportive. How did this happen? I can't help but ask myself this question over and over again. How, indeed.

All I know is that I got a letter asking me to meet with some representatives of what they called the NPO. I gathered it was some kind of business venture and decided to see what it was all about. But I was definitely not prepared for what it all entailed. I was surprised to find both adults and what I thought were children at the meeting. I found out, later, that they were elves.

Even now, my head is reeling at this crazy chance. I'm not sure if it's a dream come true, or a nightmare gone wrong. Either way, I can't help but think that I was somehow meant for this calling, because that's what I see it as, a calling. I won't get any monetary pay, but I know that I will have my own reward for this work. And to think that now I get to work with, and for, children for the rest of my life. I think that's part of why Elena came with me, because she can't have children. But this way she can be like a mother to them all.

SANTA OBSERVED Marie from the doorway for a few minutes as she read. Seeing her on the first few pages, he felt disinclined to interrupt. He felt it was rude to just stand in the doorway so he cleared his throat, smiling when she looked up. "Good evening."

Marie looked around, flustered. "Santa, I didn't expect anyone to come here." Now that she thought about it, there were several pictures of men on the walls. She realized they represented the many men who had taken on the mantle of Santa Claus. The thought came to her that this room might have been empty for a reason. "I didn't mean to intrude on your private sanctuary." She put the book down and started for the door, feeling embarrassed.

Santa laughed. "This library, and all the rooms in it, are open to all elves, and humans alike. In fact, they're open to any who live or work within the confines of the North Pole Organization. Much like yourself, I was only looking for a book to read." He picked up her discarded volume and turned it over. "I remember this one well," he continued conversationally. "It has to be some time since I last had a chance to read it. I've started a journal of my own since then. Some day, another Santa will read it, just like I read this one. Or, perhaps another elf seeking guidance?" His eyes twinkled.

"I didn't know what it was about," Marie apologized. "I just picked it up."

The Head Elf walked up to her and pressed the book into her hands. "Maybe it will make for a bit of light reading," he smiled. "I can read it some other time." He patted her on the back and walked out of the room.

Marie held the book tightly to her chest and stared after Santa's retreating form. Once he was gone, she turned the book over and over in her hands before finally returning to the Main Office Complex.

SEVEN

RACHEL REMOVED THE stethoscope from her ears and put it back in her lab coat pocket. She jotted something down on Marie's chart before turning to face her patient. "Looks like you're doing better. I don't like the puffiness around your eyes though. Means your not getting enough sleep."

Marie's face twitched as she blinked to keep her eyes open. "I've been doing a lot of studying, accompanied by a lot of homework," she admitted.

Rachel raised her eyebrows and tapped the pen on the chart. "Just what kind of schedule have you been keeping, exactly?"

Marie slumped over. "Well, I've been up at around five every morning so I can study with Clarence. He keeps me until noon when I break for lunch. Then, from about one to eight in the evening, I'm studying with him again. After that, I do whatever I need to get done," Marie replied. "I seem to be getting to bed around eleven or midnight."

Rachel continued to tap her pen on the clipboard. "That's only about five hours of sleep, at most. Clarence should know better than to keep you on a schedule like that. And you should know better than to stay up so late.

I'll have to have a little chat with him."

Marie stood from the examining table. "Please don't. I don't want to get into any kind of trouble with him. He doesn't need any more reasons to hate me."

"Trouble?" Rachel snorted. "He'll be the one in trouble if he doesn't calm down. I may deem you fit for active duty, but that doesn't give him the right to put you back in here with his stupid antics. He knows better than that." She laughed without humor. "I suppose he wants you to come back as soon as I'm finished with you."

Marie nodded. "Pretty much."

Rachel acknowledged her answer with a sigh. "All right then. I won't detain you any longer, but don't let him boss you around. You're a grown woman. You have rights too. Do him good to have someone stand up to him."

A grown woman. Marie walked out of the medical wing with her shoulders slumped. *As far as he's concerned, I'm only a puppet or a bug he can torment and squish with his shoe.*

MARIE RETURNED to the classroom in low spirits. She sat down without a word to her instructor. Pulling out a notebook and pen, she made ready for another session of mindless copying and memorization.

"Well?" Clarence fixed his gaze on her and drummed his fingers against the lectern. It almost felt like he hadn't moved from that spot. "What did Rachel say?"

"I'll live," she replied without looking up.

"Good."

"If you don't drive me into the ground, that is." Marie glared up at him, pencil in one clenched fist.

Clarence snorted. Rachel would likely bawl him out later, but he'd be one up on everyone before then. "I've decided it's time to take you on that sleigh ride Santa mentioned." He walked over to her, motioning for her to follow.

"Excuse me?" She stared after him in shock. "You mean now?"

"No, I mean tomorrow," Clarence spat. "Hurry up." He headed out the door of the lecture hall and down the corridor, not waiting to see if she was coming along or not. "I've had them get the reindeer ready while you were playing around."

Marie clenched her teeth as she followed. They walked down several different hallways and into the open, where they took a trolley to the stables. It took almost all her resolve to not show any fear as she boarded, then left the trolley behind. Clarence, on the other hand, swung on and off the contraption with practiced ease. He almost made it look like a form of art.

"This way," he said in a loud voice as they entered the building they'd been aiming for. Once inside, he handed her a long cloak and a pair of thick gloves. "Put those on. You'll need them. And just so you know, it takes a lot of effort to get the sleigh out so I hope you appreciate it. I'm sure this little venture will set back several schedules by at least three hours."

Marie frowned but stalked after him as they passed several empty stalls. They were heading towards the back of the building where a tunnel began. It led up a steep incline to the outer level. She secured the cloak around her shoulders. As she walked, she tried to keep her mind on other things, knowing that this was to be more than just an outing. It was a test, and she hoped more than anything to pass it. Clarence didn't need anything else to complain about. If she did fail, he would definitely have something nasty to say about it.

SNOW FELL and the wind blew. Marie looked through the swirling flakes and saw the green sleigh waiting to fly. In the splendor of the moment, she almost forgot why they were there. "Everything looks so different up here," she breathed in awe. *You'd never know there was a city under us, if you can call it a city*, she thought. *It's more like a different world down there.*

Clarence paused in front of the sleigh, breathing in the cold air. There was something thrilling about the prospect of flying. Maybe it was because he didn't usually get the chance to lead the reindeer team. Whatever the reason, for one brief moment, he felt completely at peace. The world around him looked like the wonderland he remembered from his childhood. The memory made the corners of his lips turn upwards just a little.

Marie resisted the urge to shuffle her feet, wondering why he was just standing there with his eyes closed. Was he imagining her freaking out over the ride, thinking about how he could use it later to further torment her? No. She shouldn't think that way. Maybe he was just admiring the view, obscured as it was. "Are you sure this is a good idea? After all, it's snowing like crazy out here. What if we hit something?"

"I think you're thinking too much," Clarence rebuked as he got back down to business. "Now pay attention." He introduced her to the reindeer, all which stared at her with big somber eyes. He didn't offer to help her into the sleigh.

"All right," he called over the breeze while he settled himself in his seat, "Don't try to grab the reins. This is only to give you a taste of flying to see if you can stomach it. I don't want any screaming or grabbing. Just keep your hands to yourself and we won't have any problems." He glanced over to make sure she understood.

Marie nodded back with uncertainty, her stomach wrenching into knots now that they were in the sleigh. "I'm not sure I can handle this at the moment," she admitted. "I've had bad experiences with heights, real bad ones." Her face contorted in worry and she looked behind her, just to make sure no one was there.

Clarence guessed at her fear with annoyance. He could feel that she was more tense than usual. "There's nothing to worry about. I'm an expert driver. You won't get dumped out. Everyone gets chills their first sleigh ride. It will go away." He almost felt sorry for her. Almost.

She glanced away, refusing to look his direction. "I wish I had your confidence. I never fancied falling thousands of feet to my death." She wished, in vain, for a seat belt.

Clarence sighed in exasperation. "Don't think about that. Like I said, it's not like you'll get dumped out or anything. Just pay attention to the signals I give the reindeer. I'll test you on them later." He called out a series of staccato notes as he held the reins. The harness tightened in his grip and the reindeer tensed. They were off with the next set of notes.

Marie gulped down a scream of terror, her stomach lurching with the sudden forward thrust. The urge to hurl was overwhelming. Her hand went to her mouth and she turned towards the side of the sleigh, just in case.

"You're not going to throw-up, are you?" He gave her a look and prodded the reins, urging the reindeer to go faster, just to see what she'd do.

She shook her head. *He's mocking me, but I won't give him the satisfaction.* She swallowed and moved her hands back to her sides. She had to clamp her hands to the edge of the sleigh for the rest of the ride, but she didn't throw up. She could say that much at least, but she was dizzy and felt sure her face was green by the time they finally landed. She slithered from the sleigh once everything had stopped moving. Even after they'd landed, she still wasn't quite sure that they'd arrived back on solid ground.

Clarence let out another exasperated sigh. He reached out just in time to steady her, keeping her from falling over. Her skin was so soft, so smooth to the touch. At least that's what his brain told him, subconsciously remembering the moment he'd first laid eyes on her. He withdrew his hand, mentally scolding himself for wanting to keep physical contact.

"I want you to memorize those commands. Maybe you won't make the same blunders others have. Now, go back in before you freeze to death." He resisted the urge to push her along. "You're dismissed for the rest of the day."

Marie hurried off before he could change his mind, praying she'd find a bathroom before her stomach rebelled any further.

DENA RAN into Marie near the ever-lit Christmas tree in the Main Rotunda. She'd learned about the surprise flight from one of the stable workers. Seeing her friend, she gave an encouraging smile, hoping to disperse the haunted look she saw in her friend's eyes. "So, how did your first flight go? I know that I'd never have enough guts to go up there."

Marie shrugged, trying not to show the fear she'd felt. She felt a bit better after having visited the lady's room. "It wasn't too bad. I almost lost my lunch. Almost. I managed to force it back down after Clarence gave me a look."

Dena nodded with sympathy. The Head of Operations was a formidable individual when he chose to be. She knew because she had locked horns with him several times before. Things always got interesting when that happened.

Marie bit her lip. She tried hard not to remember the feeling of landing, with the sleigh rushing towards the ground at an alarming speed. It was possible that Clarence had driven the reindeer towards the Arctic ice at such speeds on purpose.

A shudder ran down her spine, one she couldn't hide. Realizing she'd given herself away, she tried to not humiliate herself further by breaking down into tears. "To be honest, it was horrible. He makes it seem so simple. I felt like the world's biggest baby. I'm still shaking from it."

Dena released a silent sigh, glad that her friend had admitted to the fear and trembling she felt pouring off of her. "Yeah. It was stupid of him to spring that on you like that. I'll talk to Santa about it."

Marie shook her head, face pale. "Please don't. It's not his fault! I mean you know I have a fear of heights, but that doesn't mean he does." She didn't express how afraid she was that any more comments on his behavior would cause further hurt to her in the future.

Dena frowned. What Clarence was doing was wrong, and she was sure he knew it. But Marie was also right. If anyone brought it up, the poor girl would get even more of the same treatment. Chances were that nothing would change that. Unless there was some way to prove that Marie wasn't the criminal he suspected she was. That was indeed a shame because she was far from convinced that it was in Marie's character.

Marie glanced at the large grandfather clock hanging over the ever-burning fireplace. She noted the position of the large black hands, feeling more tired than she had before. She still had to study the material given her before visiting Rachel that morning. Even though Clarence had dismissed her early, there was still more than enough in her notes that needed to be committed to memory. Chances were that it would take all night.

Dena nodded to herself. The look on her friend's face, and Rachel's report, more than confirmed that a break was in order. She took Marie by the arm and steered her towards the main entrance of the building. "No more work for you tonight. You're taking the night off, and I don't care what Clarence thinks or says about it. We're going out and you are going to enjoy yourself if it kills me."

EIGHT

DAYS STARTED TO pass in a blur. Within what seemed like a blink of an eye, three weeks had passed. There was not so much as a hint that Clarence knew about Marie's much-needed excursion with Dena. And thanks to Dena's, and a few other elves' help, Marie could now navigate her own way through at least the central part of the city. There were also plenty of elves willing to help her if she got lost.

Clarence's lessons started to sink in too. She was relieved that she could remember at least half of what he droned at her. She knew that anything less than perfection would bring a sharp rebuke from him. She'd had the misfortune of misquoting something back to him during one particular lecture. That had resulted the most severe dressing down she'd ever had. It was completely unfair, but she'd learned to answer to his satisfaction.

What made it worse were all the new responsibilities heaped upon her. Clarence finally deemed her ready to move up in her new role as Replacement Specialist. As such, she had started her rounds of inspection with him. This meant she had to spend even more time with him as they made the rounds of each department. He was watching for any potential mistakes, more than ready to let her hear about them later.

These rounds usually ended at the Post, where a report of all incoming mail was prepared to pass on to the Head Elf. Usually, this report consisted of a list of requests from the children around the world. Invoices from the outlying outposts or outside suppliers were also noted. Such invoices were usually sent to the filing department. Sometimes there were letters that needed to be passed on with the reports. Usually, they just needed the Head Elf's attention, but some were far more sinister.

Since the beginning of the year, the staff had noted a slight increase in threatening letters. Ever since Marie had started working there, the volume of those letters had increased. As part of her duties, she was required to read those letters. Their contents only added to the silent misgivings she still felt about being there. Whoever was writing those letters had a grudge against the whole North Pole Organization. They kept hinting that something bad was going to happen soon, never telling what that would be.

Marie didn't like the idea that someone was threatening the place she was coming to love. It was almost enough to send her back into a frenzy of realistic nightmares. Half were memory, the other half pure fantasy. More often than not, she would wake in a cold sweat, panting, unable to quite remember what she'd dreamed, fearing the worst. But she had to keep this to herself and not show her misgivings when she accepted the letters from the Post. Nor could she share her misgivings when she delivered the threatening letters to Santa's office. It didn't matter that her heart beat just that much faster, her past hiding just behind the next shadow, waiting to pounce back out at her.

It was after one long day of looking over her shoulder that Marie found herself with another much needed afternoon off. The pace she'd been forced to keep was wearing on her and it showed. The mornings had been devoted to training. And with the afternoons being reserved for slugging through inspections, her free time was short. More often than not, she spent that free time trying to catch up on either sleep or studies, whichever won over first. But now, with the whole afternoon off, her mind kept turning to the threatening letters, and to fragmented visions of her past.

To stave off further thoughts of her fears, she poured over some reports. Clarence would likely want her to hand them over the moment he realized she had them. After about the first page, Marie opened her window to let in a bit more air, taking a bit of a break from the humdrum. The fresh breeze helped and she moved back to her desk to read some more but couldn't concentrate.

Conversation from Santa's office, one story below her window, drifted in with the cool air. Santa was having some kind of discussion with Clarence. She'd recognize the H.O.'s voice anywhere. She couldn't make out the words, but the sound of their voices was enough to distract her from the report. They were arguing, or at least Clarence was. His voice was the loudest, not that she could make out the words.

Trying to drown out the noise, she shut the window and forced herself to concentrate on reading the report. When that didn't work, she tried reading the journal borrowed from the library. The words just wouldn't stick in her mind so she put the book down. She found herself reopening the window because it was stuffy. She tried to listen to the conversation below by leaning out over the slight ledge. That didn't work well either.

"I give up!" She grabbed the book and headed for the library, knowing that building would hold the silence she sought. The report would have to wait.

MARIE STORMED down the stairs. Four weeks of intensive training and handshaking had sprung almost every nerve in her to the point of breaking. The training was sticking. The names weren't. She had no idea how she'd be able to remember them all. Clarence seemed to have no trouble with it.

Marie finally reached the library, after what seemed like the longest walk of her life. Everything swirled in her head, the threats, the dreams, and the argument she'd overheard. After pacing a few times in front of the large structure, she calmed down enough to go inside. It took some time to find an out of the way corner with a quiet nook. Once she found one, she settled down into a soft chair. Taking a deep breath, and hoping for some comfort, she opened up the journal she'd brought with her.

December 23, 1967

Christmas Eve is here and I've had this position for almost a year. This will be my first time making the deliveries. Hard to believe it's been that long already. So much has changed. I wonder what has happened to my friends since I've been gone. I remember a David Dovan in particular, who, though a little younger than me, has always been a good friend. His son, I can't recall the name. Was it Dylan? Damien? I can't quite seem to remember. What ever his name is, he has to be a teenager by now, almost old enough to drive, if I remember correctly. He used to be such a nice boy when he was younger.

I don't know what's going on with him, but I noticed he's marked down for coal this year. He's done some things I'm sure his father isn't proud of, which is a shame. He tried to follow me here earlier this year. I don't know why, but he feels like I betrayed his father, who I brought here once, just to prove I wasn't insane. A mistake on my part. Poor kid. Looks like he's had a rough year. I just hope nothing bad comes of this.

Dovan. The name tugged at her like an omen, leaving her feeling cold inside. Uncle Dovan? She didn't know if this was the same man. Perhaps he was the son mentioned, or someone else? How old would that boy be now? The idea that it might be one and the same, or even someone just related, sent chills up her spine. It wasn't all that common a name.

The book slipped to her lap, the pages still open as she stared into space, remembering, but not remembering. Life before waking up in the North Pole, before everything leading up to her parents' deaths, had seemed so simple. Trying to think back to that time was hard. It was like a looking at a dark blur of colors that held no real meaning. It hurt to try and find one.

CLARENCE PACED Santa's office like a caged animal waiting for the door to open so he could run free. He raked fingers through his hair. "I just don't know how much more of this I can handle," he admitted.

Santa remained seated behind his desk as he waited for his friend to finish his tirade about Marie's most recent wrong doings. The things he complained about were trivial on many levels. They ranged from not knowing where certain reports went, to not being able to handle a single flight in the sleigh. They'd been through that one already. Several times, in fact. The added input from Dena that the girl really was afraid of heights hadn't swayed the irate elf's stance one bit.

Clarence turned to face his superior, face red from his ranting. "I just keep feeling like she's jumping at shadows, and it makes me more edgy than I already am. It's maddening. There's something wrong with her, and you and I both know it! This whole thing was a big mistake."

Santa watched his Head of Operations, content to stay seated. "That may be true," he sighed, "but not for the reasons you're thinking. I should have thought to put her with someone more willing to be open. Perhaps someone like Dena. I'm hearing many good things from her."

Clarence snorted. "Of course you are! Dena's more than determined to like her. It almost goes against her nature to hate someone. Have you seen her lately? She practically fawns over her new friend." He turned in disgust, arms folded over his chest.

The Head Elf resisted the urge to roll his eyes. Clarence sounded like so many young children throwing a tantrum that it wasn't even funny. "And yet," Santa interjected, "Dena has been the best, most reliable security chief we've had. She is able to tell when a person is lying without even having to so much as bat an eye. Her instincts are that sound. I admit it's true that I do give her a lot more of a free hand than I do others. But what she is doing with Marie is under my direct supervision, and for a specific reason."

The younger looking man bowed his head in partial submission. After all, what his superior had said about Dena's abilities was true. Why he kept trying to discount them with Marie was beyond him. Even he wasn't sure of any a rational reason behind that. Maybe it was just a feeling. But Dena was respectable, and more than trustworthy. Unfortunately, he knew that Santa was aware of his prejudice and would have nothing to do with it. "If you say so," he sulked.

Santa smiled. "The answers you and I are both seeking will be found in time," he assured, coming around to put a hand on his friend's shoulder. "Patience is required on both our parts. Besides, we have more pressing matters."

Clarence looked up, not sure what he meant until Santa pointed to the pile of letters on his desk. They were all from the same anonymous source. And they all threatened that some kind of retribution was coming, giving no idea of when or what to expect. Seeing the serious expression on the older man's face, he nodded. "I'll take those to Dena right away. Maybe she'll have some insight on them, something we've missed."

Santa handed him the stack with a sigh of resignation. "I only hope this is someone's idea of a prank, but I fear something more sinister lies behind it, though I have no idea what. While you're at it, ask Dena to tighten things up a bit more, especially around the major cities and stations."

Clarence tapped the letters. "I'll get these delivered and pass on the word."

The old man settled back into his chair with a groan as Clarence left. "I'm getting too old for this," he sighed.

MARIE STARED ahead of her. She was still unable to believe that there could be two different people with the same name, and both somehow connected with the North Pole Organization. David Dovan, the man who was a friend to the previous Santa. Could he be the one who haunted her past? Or maybe his son? She wanted to deny the possibility. It hurt too much otherwise. She was so wrapped up in her own brooding that she didn't realize that someone had entered her little corner.

"Mind if I join you," Santa asked, breaking into her thoughts.

She started from her reverie, looking up as he smiled at her. "Uh…sure." She closed the book in a hurry and set it aside. "I was just reading."

"To me, it looked as though you were a million miles away." He sat down on the closest chair. "Mind sharing?"

Marie ran a hand through her long hair. "I was just remembering," she glanced up at Santa, then back down at her lap, "looking back on the last few weeks," she clarified.

"Ah." He nodded. "They have been busy weeks for you, haven't they? Clarence has been over zealous in his training." Marie nodded, much to Santa's amusement. "He and I were just having a nice little chat about that before I came over."

She looked at the floor. "I know. I could hear his voice through the window. Not that I heard what was said," she added in a rush. "It was just distracting."

"So you came here. Understandable," Santa assured. "Clarence does have a tendency to get... overexcited at times."

Right. Is that what you call it? She twiddled her fingers. "So... did you want something?"

"I wanted to get to know you better." Santa's warm smile seemed to light the room. "The last few weeks have been so hectic. I try to get to know all my elves, you see. It's important that I have a grasp of who I'm working with. Of course I've already seen Dena's reports, and I have my own observations from the past few weeks. It hasn't been easy for you has it?"

Marie looked down at her shoes. "No, not exactly. At least not as easy as I'd have liked. I can't help but think part of it is my fault. After all, I am the only one who can dictate what I feel."

Santa nodded. "True, but you can't dictate what others do."

She looked up at that comment. "No I can't." She licked her lips. "But it's hard to not let others get to me."

"Speaking of which, don't let Clarence get to you," Santa grunted as he rearranged his legs to find a more comfortable sitting position.

"Clarence?" She stared at him, her face blank.

"Yes, Clarence," he agreed. "I've heard reports that there is an uncommon amount of tension between you two. I would prefer it if my elves didn't have any bad feelings towards each other. We are all a part of a team here. Do try to get along with him."

"I can try, but he doesn't like me," Marie responded. "Truth is, I get the feeling he hates me."

Santa's eyebrows rose at her comment. "Oh? Why do you say that?"

She took a deep breath before launching into an explanation behind her frustrations. "He's cold and distant. He never tries to get along with me. He was against me from moment one. He hates my guts."

Santa peered at her over his glasses, much like he would at a school child who had gotten into trouble. "Don't you think you're being a little unfair? Think of it coming from his eyes. I've known him a long time. He's tough, and sometimes seems hot tempered, but he's usually fair," he chided.

Marie shook her head. "Usually isn't always. He hates me. I know it."

Santa smiled with kindness. "Are you sure the feeling isn't mutual? You haven't taken the time to get to know him have you? Just try."

"But--"

Santa held up a finger to silence her. "Just try."

"All right." She sighed. "But I can't promise anything will come of it."

"That's all I ask of my elves," Santa replied. "Oh, while I'm thinking of it, I should remind you of something. On your rounds with Clarence, as someone equal in rank, you can make suggestions and executive decisions. I'm sure he may not agree with me, but don't let him order you around."

Marie sat back in her chair, looking like she was a towel someone had just thrown there. "You want me to be more assertive during my rounds with him? Santa, trying to get along with him as a teacher is hard enough. Trying to be his equal... That's asking too much."

Santa reached over and placed a hand on her shoulder. "I know it seems like a lot to ask, but I am asking it. I know what it's like to work with someone who doesn't want to accept you as an equal. That doesn't mean you can't be better than he is. I've noticed what's been going on between the two of you, and you have my sympathies, but he won't trust you unless you let him get to know you."

Marie blinked back a few tears as she shook her head. "I can't do that."

"Why not?"

"I can't. Don't you understand?" Frustrated, she went on, resisting the urge to stand and in pace the small room. "I can't even face myself in the mirror without seeing something I don't like. Without being reminded--" She stopped mid sentence. She was afraid to continue the thought, afraid of what it meant about her. She was even more afraid of the danger it placed them both in. How could she admit to the possibility that there were things from her past that could put them all in danger?

Santa turned his head, hoping she might go on without prodding. He didn't dare push; four weeks was too soon for that. *I must have patience*, he thought, nodding. "All right. I'll take you on your word that you're trying to get along with him. And please do try, Marie. We all need to be working together. Christmas may still be months off, but if we aren't prepared, things will happen that I don't care to think about."

"I wouldn't want... that is, I'll do my best." She looked back down at her clasped hands.

"Good. Just keep up a good attitude and you'll make it."

Marie yawned. "Sorry to run out on you, but I'm really tired." She stood to go, the book tucked under her arm.

"One more thing," Santa said as he stood to follow her to the door.

She stopped and turned around, hoping he wouldn't ask her to do anything else. Especially if it had anything to do with Clarence. There was no way she could anything else on that front. "Yes?"

The Head Elf smiled. "I just wondered how you liked the journal. I haven't had a chance to ask you before."

Marie thought, with some guilt, of how the book had lain unopened on her dresser for the last few weeks. "It's... good. I'm just having a hard time finding time to read it."

He nodded with a knowing look. "Just thought I'd ask."

"Anything else?" Marie asked.

"No." He watched out of the corner of his eye as Marie left the room. "You are one we will have to watch with care." He rubbed his chin in thought.

NINE

CLARENCE RESISTED THE growing urge to do something completely irrational. It was hard, though, as he watched Marie interacting with one of the Toy Department supervisors. What was it about her that just grated on his nerves? He clenched and unclenched a fist held next to his thigh. Why did everyone just seem to just like her for no reason? Was she using some kind of elf magic?

The H.O. scowled as he watched Marie listen to the supervisor. Her now bronzed hair glistened in the artificial light of the shop floor as she nodded at something the supervisor said. There was no time for personal vanity; he had made sure of that, which meant that there was no way she could have changed her hair color. There were only a few reasonable explanations, one, she'd used magic, or two, the sun's rays had dyed it that simply... delicious color. He trembled inside. He'd been contemplating that color for much longer than he'd intended.

Marie shook the supervisor's hand and turned to find Clarence, stopping in surprise as she noticed his expression. For whatever reason, he seemed to be staring off into space, deep in thought. It was definitely the first time she'd ever caught him in such a pose and she raised a brow in bemusement. "Ready to go?"

Clarence came back to himself with a quick jerk of the head. He tried to shake out his tensed hand as he moved towards her. "I've been ready, and waiting. Let's go, before we get even more behind schedule." He strode past her without a second glance, hand still trembling from the force he'd used to clench it.

Marie blinked in confusion. She wasn't sure what had just happened, but decided it was wiser to not comment as she fell into step next to him. Ever since her talk with Santa, she had tried to be more outgoing, more authoritarian. She wasn't sure if it was working, or if it was worth the effort. Clarence seemed more distant than ever. That didn't help with trying to get along with him, though it was good that he wasn't trying to put her down so much. That was a nice change to be sure.

Without paying attention to where they were going, she followed him outside. It took a moment for her to notice that he was headed towards one of the many trolley stations. Looking up, she realized he'd already boarded the car and was waiting for her. "Crap." She lunged for the closest pole. As a result, she almost missed the last step as the platform ended under her, sending her tumbling into her companion.

Clarence fell against the seat with a huff as Marie crashed into him, knocking the wind from his lungs. One of his arms automatically went around her waist to keep her from falling any further forward. He froze, eyes wide as he realized that his hand was encircling her with an almost tender touch.

Marie's eyes went wide in surprise as she found herself somehow on top of her companion, his arm around her waist. She was so shocked that all she could do was blink, her mind oddly free of all reason. His arm felt gentle around her. And intimate. It was more intimate than she'd allowed herself to get with anyone. It felt nice somehow.

Like someone had hit the play button, everything seemed to start back up again. Clarence noticed that several of the other passengers, and the elves outside of the trolley, were staring at them. He righted himself as he helped Marie back to her feet. He then brushed himself off in a very business-like manner. "You know, you really should watch where you're going," he commented in an almost snide manner.

Marie held her breath, mentally counting to ten before replying. She held back the equally snide comment that had popped into her head while calming down. "I'll keep that in mind." She took a seat next to him. She made sure there was enough room between them that they didn't touch. Turning abruptly away, her hair fanned out around her, hitting him squarely in the face.

Clarence held back a growl, deciding that her hair wasn't that pretty after all. He had to blink to keep his eyes from watering from the impact of the long strands. How could he have even thought it worth admiring, even for the smallest millisecond? Everything about this girl was lethal! He turned to face away from her, and any other possible attacks from that divine hair. He decided that the moment their rounds were over, he would take a much-needed disinfecting shower.

SANTA CLAUS frowned as he reread the report in front of him. His glasses almost fell off his nose as he peered at the pages. "This doesn't bode well. Not at all," he mused, flipping to the next page. "And it's just like last time, you say?" He peered over the rims of his glasses at his head of security.

Dena nodded with a grim frown. "Exactly like last time. No security footage, no prints. Nothing. Just some eye witness testimonies of some unknown person being there who shouldn't be, and no idea if this person was human or elf." She tapped the table-like top of her personal computer. It was similar to the one in the main Security

League office, only smaller.

Santa rubbed at his brows, putting the papers back on the desk part of the workstation. He was grateful for the comfortable chairs in Dena's private office. The added support was definitely needed after this significantly bad news. "Do we know what they were after?"

The security chief shook her head, not able to answer. "It was a remote location, with nothing major attached, except for a drop shaft to the Subway, which, I'm told, was not discovered. There are no recorded entrance or exit protocols to the Subway within the time frame of this incident. In fact, there were no log entries of any access at all. I double-checked. I've got a crew there to keep an eye on things, though. Just in case."

Santa nodded at her thoroughness. It would have been bad if the Subway's drop shaft had been discovered. It would give any intruder an almost direct link to North Pole City, or any other part of their organization for that matter. It would have been so simple to bypass all security before someone could have stopped it. It would not have been the first time, which was why many stations had been relocated in the last few years. They could not afford a repeat of the last time such an event had occurred.

The Head Elf stared at the lime green walls, focusing on the abstract art hanging in colored frames. "Does Clarence or Marie know about this?" He tapped the file on her desk with one wrinkled finger.

Dena picked up the report and slid it into one of the many drawers behind her, filing it away for later perusal. "No. I made sure this one didn't reach Clarence's ears. I had to send in a few of my personal team, but I'm pretty sure both he and Marie are in the dark on this one. And, if you ask my opinion, I think it's best that it stays that way."

Santa nodded. "I'm of the same opinion," he sighed. "I think those two might be starting to get along. Something like this is more likely to break the fragile peace between them. And I can't have that happening right now, not when things are so close to becoming better."

Dena smiled, glad that they were of the same mind on that matter, though they usually were on a similar vein anyway. "I've heard good reports," she confirmed, "and I'm hoping the same thing. They really are good for each other, if only they'd stop being so stubborn."

The elderly elf laughed at that, picturing an old married couple bickering at each other. "Whether they end up being together or not, it's good for the both of them to have someone with a little fight in them to contend with."

Dena moved around the desk to stand next to her superior. As she moved, she turned to stare at one of the security screens that showed the Main Rotunda. "There are several elves who are taking bets on who will break first, you know."

Santa turned to look at the screen as well. He caught a brief glimpse of the two in question as they left one of the buildings, before the image rotated to another view. "I can't say that I'm surprised by these developments. They're both tough nuts to crack. The question is what kind of nut is inside each shell." *And who will crack first.*

Dena groaned. "You're making me hungry with that kind of talk. Now I'll have to order something from the Kitchen." She stepped over to a smaller screen and typed in a food order. "Want anything?"

The Head elf shook his head, indicating his expansive waistline. "I'd better not. I'm having a hard time fitting into the suit as is, and I'd rather not make extra work for the tailors, if you know what I mean," he winked. "Incidentally, I did want to discuss something else before I have to return to my office."

Dena finished her order with a push of a button, turning back at the change of tone in Santa's voice. "What is it?"

Santa caught another glimpse of Marie and Clarence as the screen switched to yet another view. He pointed to the screen, "has Marie given you any more information about her past? Anything at all?"

The security chief's face fell as she shook her head. "Not really, unfortunately. At least, nothing that tells us more about what happened before she came here, or where she came from. She has confessed to being able to do small things with her magic, like opening locked doors."

Santa nodded. Most elves were able to tap into their inner magic and do things that normal people could not do. Some of those things included manipulating small bits of matter. Others included performing small acts of persuasion. Those acts usually resulted in someone being more willing to cooperate. That was the kind of magic Dena employed. Few elves worked any magic larger than that. They opted to not take the time to learn the more difficult levels of control required. That, and it took a lot out of most of them.

"It would be unusual if she didn't have some skill with her elf magic," he mused. "Especially at her age, which I'm guessing is closer to Clarence's, at least from her outer appearance."

Dena nodded agreement. "I've started looking in the older records to see if I can find any reference to anyone who looks like her. Just to see if she might have lived in any of our colonies. I've even gotten Rachel to supply some DNA for the purpose. No success yet, though."

Santa put a reassuring hand on her shoulder. "We will find it soon enough, the key to her past that will hopefully shed some light on what's going on now. Let's just hope that she opens up to us before anything else happens. I have an unsettling feeling. Despite my own personal feelings, Clarence may be right about her being somehow involved in all this." He indicated the cabinet with the file. "Even if it is unwittingly, though I definitely hope I'm wrong."

Dena stared at the screen, still showing Clarence and Marie as they walked down one of the many streets in the city. "You and me both."

JULY CAME and Marie finally found some time alone. The past few weeks had been busy. They were filled with inspections, more tutoring on her duties, and a couple of outings with Dena. Clarence had, unfortunately, interrupted one such occurrence, sending her off on some meaningless errand.

Finding herself with a free afternoon, she snuck to her room and pulled out the long ignored journal. She was a little ashamed of the layer of dust that had collected on the cover, which she wiped off before opening to a random entry.

January 1, 1978

We've just experienced what I'd call a near miss on our part. I'd heard from David that his son went missing. I had no idea he'd try to find his way here, but there he was, right in my office. I have no idea how he got in. He didn't say either. Luckily, I wasn't alone. Sandra, my secretary, was with me. She called in the Special Forces to catch the young man.

What upsets me the most is that he kept yelling at me and threatening me. I think he was relocated to a place somewhere in California. I wouldn't be surprised if he'd gone crazy. The look in his eyes would support that. I suggested placing him in an institution, for his own good. I feel bad for his father.

We've also decided to create the Security League. It makes sense to turn our Special Forces into a more formal organization. We're using the most elite for internal security. Dena was unanimously nominated for the position as head the of new League. I feel safer with her there.

Marie stopped reading, a cold chill running up her back. *This boy can't be related to Uncle Dovan,* she told herself as she pulled a blanket up around her shoulders. The thought only partially comforted her, though the words didn't completely ring true. She turned several pages and began reading again, hoping to find something to erase the fear of the name from her mind.

March 22, 1982

The Dovan boy has disappeared and it makes me feel uneasy. He'd be about twenty-eight now, I think. Local authorities searched for him without any luck. I fear the worst and have had Dena sweep the entire city several times, just to be sure he hadn't come back. Nothing. Either he's good at hiding or he's biding his time. I don't like it, but what can I do? His poor father. He still doesn't believe anything about the North Pole, despite my having shown him.

What is it about life and growing up that makes us unable to believe? Is it the onset of reality calling to us, or duty to home, family, and job security that does it? When do we reach that point where we no longer believe? For some it comes early. For others, it takes longer. And then there are some who never reach the point where they can't believe. I am grateful for them. I admit I had to be reminded. I didn't believe at first, but there have been others before me who found it harder to accept than I did.

What has Christmas become to the world? I see a growing trend that frightens me. A trend of commercializing Christmas, which is wonderful for businesses, but takes out the spirit of the season. The first Claus did not start this fine legacy to be bought out by stores, but to help the children. Christmas, in a way, is for them. It's all about the magic. It's about the giving. Where did we adults go wrong? Christmas is for the children. They know the answer. If only we could all remain as innocent and trusting as they are.

I don't know what to do about David Dovan anymore either, to be honest. These past few years, he's been rather odd, and I'm afraid he might be losing his sanity. I could be wrong about that though. At least his wife doesn't have to deal with this, though her death was not an easy one. I attended the funeral only last month. I think I mentioned it earlier. The look in his eyes is something I will never forget. I think he still blames me for her death.

What had happened to Dovan's wife, Marie wondered. Not sure if she wanted to know, but feeling that it might somehow be important, she began skimming the entries. She paused any time she saw the name Dovan even so much as hinted at. Such entries became fewer between, but she soon tired of looking. *There's no sense in chasing ghosts*, she told herself. Putting the journal down for the night, she turned off the lights.

TEN

CLARENCE CHEWED ON the end of his pen as he reread the scrawled letters in his notepad. They were just meaningless doodles that looked like notes. The real notes were locked inside his head, spinning around and round, like the wash cycle of a washing machine. Things were getting downright ridiculous, he decided, and it didn't look like they would stop any time soon. He let out a sigh, heavy with stress and frustration. It was inevitable that it would happen again. Thankfully, he'd been in the right place at the right time. After all, it was only chance that had landed him there, less than an hour after the incident.

Clarence had been on one of his usual jaunts to the different outposts. He tried to have at least one surprise inspection a week, always picking them at random. He'd planned on visiting a station in a completely different continent, but had changed his mind. He was glad, now, that he'd done so.

Elves walked around him, almost as if on eggshells, not sure if his temper would erupt or not. They all knew that he'd been rather irritable, more so than usual, for the past few weeks. This was due to the rumors someone had started, probably by a trolley worker, about his supposed involvement with Marie. And all completely unfounded! A mistake of timing was the reality of the matter. But the hushed gossip told him the story was being publicized as something completely different.

Clarence had been bent on making sure such rumors were left unfounded. He had done everything in his power to put distance between himself and his associate. He did his best to keep strictly professional, schooling any thoughts to the contrary so that no more rumors could be formed. Every time he'd heard such a rumor, Clarence erupted in what could only be categorized as a miniature vent of temper. Such outbursts had left several younger elves on the verge of tears. Santa had chastised him, of course, but that didn't help matters.

With great effort, Clarence turned his thoughts away from the gossip. He was glad that Marie wasn't anywhere near the vicinity. Instead, she was enjoying a day off with Dena, which was just as well. He didn't need either of them getting involved in this before he had a chance to try and sort everything out. Even if it wasn't his job to do so. With another scowl, he removed the mangled pen from his mouth and prepared to take more notes. "And you say that no one saw this person? No security footage whatsoever?"

The supervisor of the Texas outpost shook her head. Her short hair flew out from her face in a somewhat similar manner to what Marie could achieve, though it wasn't nearly as impressive with her shorter locks. "No footage, no tampering of the Subway drop shaft, though I do have an elf who thinks they may have seen something."

Clarence mentally perked at that, but only showed it by narrowing his eyes a bit, and furrowing his brow. "Oh? Who was that? And what did they see?"

The supervisor pointed to a younger elf with the appearance of a five-year-old boy. He stepped out from behind the relative protection of a rather tall plant, looking anxious. "Tell him what you saw," she encouraged with a gentle nudge.

The lad swallowed and tried to wet his lips. "I was doing a check on one of the control assemblies for the drop shaft," he said with a tight voice before clearing his throat to continue. "I'd just crawled into an access hatch when I heard footsteps. I knew no one was supposed to be there so I turned as best I could to see who it was, thinking one of my friends was going to try and scare me. It happens a lot. Them trying to scare me, I mean. Not the footsteps," he admitted. "I realized that whoever it was, didn't belong there."

Clarence lifted a brow, not relaxing his interrogator's grim expression for even a nanosecond. He tried to digest and filter though this new information. "And?"

The technician swallowed again. "Well, uh… I noticed that the shoes were too big for an elf. We don't have any humans in this station, so I knew it was someone who shouldn't be there. I think they were wearing jeans, but since I was looking over my shoulder, trying not to get noticed, I'm not sure. Never saw anything past the legs, but I beeped in the alarm. Seemed to know something was up, though, as he left the room."

The Head of Operations chewed the inside of his lip. He was frustrated that more information hadn't been gathered. He was pleased that at least something had finally been discovered about this perpetual intruder. That, of course, was assuming that it was the same person. "And are you sure this person was male?"

The lad nodded. "Men's shoes, size eleven, sneakers of some kind, with long legs. His knees came to about where my view ended because of the hatchway. My senses say he was closer to six feet tall, maybe a bit less."

The supervisor nodded as the technician was allowed to leave. "Fredrick's elf magic excels in judging sizes and other special reasoning. I have no doubt that what he's said is accurate."

Clarence nodded. It was definitely something, which was better than nothing, he mused. But how could an almost six foot tall man make his way into one of the more well guarded outposts? And without triggering internal, or external alarms? Furthermore, why was there no footage of the fact? He didn't like it, not one bit.

Sliding the notepad into his pocket, he put the pen back on the desk of the small office he'd borrowed for the occasion. Somehow, this all felt like a waste of time and he almost wished he'd included Marie on this trip. She had a way of picking up on things that he somehow missed, though he doubted she'd find anything else. It would have been nice to have someone he could mull this over with, though, someone who could tell him to stop going over too many details. Someone who could pull him back and help him see the bigger picture.

He dashed the thought aside, shocked that he'd let her back into his thoughts so casually. Since when had he valued her input so much? He was still wasn't sure if he trusted her or not, despite her good opinions, common sense, and good looks. No, it was better that she wasn't there, he decided, for both of them. These elves didn't need anything else to add to the rumor mill.

"Let me know if anything else comes up. Or if anyone else remembers anything suspicious," he instructed as he moved away from the borrowed desk. "Keep your ears open, and if you so much as hear anything that could help, send it my way."

The supervisor nodded in agreement, showing him back to the drop shaft, more than ready to have the Head of Operations back on his way. She did not wave as the shaft's door sealed behind her guest, but let out a sigh, wondering what else could upset her day's work.

DENA FROWNED at the display screen in front of her. She still could not find a single frame that showed their mysterious intruder. Even after having gone through all the footage for all three break-ins at least ten or more times. Thanks to Clarence's report, they did have more to go on. But without that important video evidence, the information wasn't hugely helpful.

The chief rubbed her eyes with one hand, tapping out commands on her computer with the other. Having access to the entire grid of information did help in trying to determine just what their intruder was after. But it was slow and tedious work. She would rather have handed the task over to a junior officer. Unfortunately, Dena wasn't sure that she dared do that. It increased the possibility of missing something important. There just had to be some corresponding data to tell them what was going on. And it had to be something outside of the actual intrusions that had occurred in much the same manner.

"This isn't working," she groaned as she ran slim fingers through her hair. "I still can't figure out what they're after." She just hoped that after this last time, having been seen by someone would be deterrent enough to end this long nightmare.

Time was getting tight, with production at its peak. They couldn't afford to have something happen, not in the second half of the year. Not like this. And most definitely not like last time there had been an intrusion at North Pole City. Dena didn't think anyone, new or seasoned, could take something like that. She hoped and prayed they wouldn't have to do so. It would likely undo all the good she'd worked so hard to do, especially between Clarence and Marie. If Marie were somehow involved... She wouldn't think about it.

AUGUST HAD been a long and exhausting month and had passed slowly. It had been filled with more pointless education in the ways of the elves, not that Marie needed it. Some things just seemed to pop into place without her even having to think about it. But she put that all aside as she stared out at the frozen landscape of the North Pole tundra.

September, in contrast, was always a pretty month in

the wide plains and fields out in the "human" world. With touches of green and brown here and there, even near the end of the month, it was breathtaking. Marie missed those flat stretches now. She remembered the cool breezes as they flew down the trees and played with the falling leaves. There were no leaves here to play in.

Marie had been working hard for months, doing her best to try and get along with Clarence as requested. He wasn't making things easy. His continued coldness towards her was unnerving, especially since she didn't understand why. Sure, she got the point that he suspected she was behind all the letters and intrusions. He had made that perfectly clear from moment one, even if he hadn't said anything about it lately. But that didn't explain all the other odd looks, and occasional remarks, he sent her way. Not to mention some of his more recent odd behavior.

Marie brushed off an odd sort of chill that came when she thought about his continued attitude. And just when she'd thought things were starting to get better. Everything had definitely been different before that unfortunate incident on the trolley. Thinking about it made her feel so tired that she longed for a place to lie down and sleep.

Everything was in constant motion and August had kept her more than busy. She'd rushed from here to there, visiting some of the more outlying parts of the North Pole Organization. At least she hadn't been asked to visit the southern continents. Unfortunately, this meant that she had to do a lot more work. She had to learn more elves' names, visit more facilities, inspect more work, and read a lot more reports. Somehow, she'd managed to keep up with everything. She was happy to learn that this was not to be a usual part of her duties. The various supervisors would eventually send their reports to her instead of her having to go out and get them.

With the increasing pace, there had been little time for personal recreation, let alone a decent night's sleep. It was all beginning to take its toll on her. In an odd moment away from her usual partner, she found herself walking down one of the long corridors of the Main Office Complex. It was somewhere near the less traversed areas.

The benches that were placed down this stretch were so tempting. They had a bit of padding on the hardwood surfaces, making them perfect for a small break. Settling wearily into one such cushion, Marie couldn't refuse the inviting call of sleep that overcame her. Her body only wanted to rest for a minute. That minute turned into hours and Clarence came looking for her.

Marie walked down a long tunnel, voices calling after her, ghostly faces swimming before her eyes like cobwebs. They were faces she once knew and didn't want to remember now. She tried to brush them away, like the wisps of nothing they were, but they stuck to her fingers like spider silk. She was at the bottom of a deep stairwell, cement and steel. And above her, a framework of a warehouse, crates stacked to the girders. She slowly climbed the stairs, looking behind her at every step, afraid. Something was in the shadows as she slipped behind some crates.

A loud noise startled her and she turned to see the cause, only to stare into a pair of eyes so dreadful that she gasped. They were bloodshot and intent, manic eyes that followed her and always knew where she was. She turned around and ran down a walkway. Although it seemed long, it ended within heartbeats, suddenly changing into stairs. She struggled upward, feeling like she'd been running for ages. The stairs didn't want to end, unlike the hall below.

An icy breath felt for her neck and she tried not to heed it. The landing finally appeared. Cold air whipped around her and she ran towards the cold through an open doorway at the end of the short runway. She raced through, finding herself on the roof, kicking up drifts of powdery snow. The ground ended abruptly underneath her. Her feet felt for solid ground as she turned around.

Cold eyes met hers. A steel barrel rose to meet her frantic gaze, one that she knew all to well. The late afternoon light glinted off of its metal casing. A shot rang out and she screamed.

Marie rocked back and forth, hot tears rolling down her cheeks. Her knees were pulled up to her trembling chest. She clutched at her left shoulder, protecting her body by covering her chest with one arm. Her open eyes saw nothing but black sky and falling snow.

"It's okay."

The voice came from a distance, almost as if from a deep pool of water. "It's okay." Someone was rocking her trembling body. A hand moved hers from the searing pain and she flinched. Her hand left minute amounts of moisture on the one that now held it. "It was only a dream. It's okay."

But her unfocused eyes saw blood on her hand and a man's face laughing at her. She couldn't hear his laughter, though. Her ears were deafened by the loud report of the firearm. She closed her eyes and buried her face into the warm shoulder that held her, turning to do so. Tears streamed down her face.

"No, no, no," she whispered. "Please no." She groaned as he removed her other hand from her chest. Both hands were bright red in her eyes. She grabbed at him like one would a lifeline, hyperventilating, not recognizing who he was.

Clarence disengaged her arms from his body, trying to stand up. The wooden bench only accounted for half his discomfort. He didn't know what to do. He wanted to help, but something held him back, personal feelings perhaps. It was her eyes that haunted him the most, and her screaming. He didn't know what had gotten into him to hold her as he had. It had nothing to do with how much he felt attracted to her, regardless of how much he tried to deny it.

Marie blinked a few times, the wisps of nightmare falling from her eyes. She saw Clarence and went rigid with shock, pulling away. "I..." Was this part of the dream? If so, she wasn't sure if she wanted it to end.

"What happened?" The ground under him was heaving,

like his thoughts. "Are you...?"

She refused to give him a chance to finish, realizing it couldn't be real. The concern in his eyes. The tenderness of his touch. She stood with some effort, pushing his hands away. "I'm sorry. So sorry," she whispered through her tears. If this was real, she couldn't afford to let it last. She couldn't let anyone get close to her, no matter how much she wished she could. She pushed away from Clarence and ran down the hall.

Clarence stared after her retreating form, noticing that she clutched at one shoulder as if in pain. His head spun. He couldn't think clearly. Why was she acting like that? What had he just done? Why had he comforted someone he didn't know anything about? He didn't know who she really was, after all. Wasn't he looking for her? He couldn't remember.

ELEVEN

CLARENCE SLUMPED OVER the balcony railing, downcast eyes surveying the streets below Santa's office. They were busy, but not any busier than his thoughts. He wished he had a handkerchief to blot the red from his eyes.

Santa watched him from inside the glass doorway. He hadn't seen his elf look this down in a long time. "Clarence," he went out onto the balcony, "what's wrong?"

Clarence turned to look at him, arms resting heavily on the railing. His eyes hid tears that were ready to fall. "I don't know," he shook his head. "I don't know what happened. I heard her scream. She was just lying there on the bench, and then she sat up and screamed. I felt as if she must have just experienced something terrible. Something in her eyes just… I don't know."

He turned his back to the railing and leaned against it, shutting out the sight of the city below. "I wanted to do something to comfort her, but I didn't know what to do. I found myself rocking her like my father used to when I was frightened at night. The next thing I knew, she was running away from me." His face showed a distress and helplessness that broke Santa's heart. "And I don't understand why."

"Do you know what happened? Did you try to talk to her?" Santa looked at him with concern. He knew full well that his Head of Operations wouldn't have thought to go after her, not in his confused state. "Is there anything I can do?"

Clarence shook his head. "It must have been a dream; a dream that could wake you up at night, screaming for dear life." He shuddered, images from his own nightmares reflected behind his eyelids. "No, I couldn't talk to her. I was so confused. I don't even know what I'm going to do about it. She scares me, Santa. She scares me to death. There's something about her that just sticks to you that you can't wash it off, no matter how hard you try. And I don't know if it's a good or a bad thing."

Santa gave him an odd look. "Clarence, there is something we haven't exactly discussed."

The elf looked up in surprise. He wondered if, somehow, this wizened man had seen something about his relationship with Marie that he hadn't. Or, perhaps, something that had upset him. It wouldn't have been the first time something had done so, but he was unprepared for Santa's next comment.

"Have you ever noticed how much Marie usually keeps to herself? It's almost as if she's afraid of contaminating everyone, as if she were afraid of everyone else. She only acts naturally around Dena. I'm not the only one who's noticed it either. It concerns me, even though she has made some friends."

"I..." Clarence hesitated. "I guess I have noticed, but didn't let myself think about it. I've been trying to avoid her." He sighed in relief for finally let it out. "I feel odd when I'm around her. It confuses me more than anything else does. At first, I was full of suspicion about her. You have to admit, the circumstances around finding her were odd," he inserted. "I mean, threats from an unknown person against you and the rest of us. Then she shows up out of the blue. Not to mention her first reaction to me."

Santa nodded sadly. "Yes, I recall your reactions, your suspicions. I can't say I ever felt your apprehension. It was more a sense that something would happen if I took her in. She's not a criminal, Clarence."

"I know," the elf sighed, his heart a stone in his chest. He wasn't sure when it had happened, but his idea of her had slowly changed. She was no longer the suspect he'd thought she was. "I've slowly felt my mind changing about her. I didn't want to accept it. It was easier to mistrust and hate her."

Santa shook his head, "Hate is an easy emotion to hold on to. It takes a strong person to let that hate go. It takes an even stronger person to not hate in the first place. But, after all, human, or elf, nature does play into all this." He walked over to the railing and looked down on the city. "And you said you'd felt a change in how you see her."

"Yes." Clarence ran a hand through his hair. "I always seem to say something, or do something really stupid when she's around. Some snide comment that I wouldn't have said a few months ago just pops out, or a look I can't even begin to fathom. It just doesn't seem to make sense to me why I do it. I don't understand her. I don't understand me when I'm around her. It's like there is a puzzle there, but all the pieces are hidden, or turned over or something so that I can't see them."

Santa patted his shoulder, nodding in understanding. "I know what you're going through. It's not going to be easy, but you must ignore it. You have obligations you need to take care of. I want you to take her on another try at the sleigh. It's been a while. Let her fly this time. She's ready. And keep an eye on her reactions. See how much she's learned. Then report back to me about your observations. But, just so you are aware, I may not be in my office as much. It seems that there are some things I have ignored for far too long."

"Ignored?" Clarence questioned, pushing himself away

from the railing. "What have you ignored?"

Santa sighed as he leaned on the doorframe. "From the moment Marie first came here, the exact moment mind you, I have kept my eyes and ears open. There is a mystery about her that one can't see, but can feel. She has obviously had something happen to her, but what I don't know. We must find out. I fear that her coming here was no accident. There is something far more sinister behind all this. Call it intuition if you will, but I feel she holds something that could either destroy us all, or save us. There is only one problem. She doesn't tell anyone about anything that has happened to her, and I'm sure that that is a part of it. I have let it lie, afraid of hurting her, but it seems I have let it sit for far too long." Santa looked out over the city, deep in thought.

Clarence looked at the Head Elf. "So, all those times you had me report on her activities was for the benefit of trying to figure her out? All those outings she had with Dena? The position that you placed her in, even though I wasn't serious in suggesting it? It was all just to unlock some deep secret she's kept hidden from the world?"

"I would say still keeps hidden," Santa interrupted. "I know only a little more about her since I first met her, but it's not enough. And not all those outings with Dena were for information gathering. We all want Marie to be able to fit in here. She's easy to get along with. Everyone else already adores her."

Clarence hesitated to voice the next thought on his mind, but knew he needed to mention it. "Um… there's something you should probably know. When I found her…" he paused, swallowing. "When she ran from me, she was clutching at her shoulder as if she were in pain."

Santa nodded, contemplating in silence for a moment. "Rachel said she'd noticed some scar tissue around her left shoulder, closer to her heart. She believes it came from some kind of puncture wound. She wasn't sure what had caused it." He hoped his H.O. wouldn't question that.

Knowing someone had shot Marie might be too much for him to handle at the moment.

Clarence tapped his chin, his thoughts turning inward. He'd never had the opportunity to see any of the medical charts that would have disclosed this information, nor had he seen the scar tissue. "Why wasn't I told?"

Santa shrugged. "At the time, I didn't think you'd see it in the same light I did. And once she was awake... well, it just didn't seem to matter if you were told or not. But I hope that this knowledge will give you greater incentive to try and help her, instead of treating her the way you have. Don't think I'm unaware of it."

Clarence hung his head in shame. "I admit that I have often felt intimidated by her. And sometimes I just can't help but want to scream at her and force her to tell me things I know she is holding back from me."

"From us all," Santa reminded. "She's had a hard life. You can tell. But we must be patient. It's wiser to keep focused on the here and now. Take her on the sleigh ride, and let her have the reins," Santa reminded. "Watch her closely. From what you told me about her first flight, you will likely find some interesting things worth reporting. Think of it as an opportunity to test her knowledge."

"All right," Clarence conceded. "But I can't schedule it in for a while. It's the busy season, as you know. It won't be long until December and we all know what that means. Don't worry, I'll fit it in," he added, catching the look in Santa's eye. "I will. I promise."

December 23, 1997

I've been afraid that something is coming, some horrible event. I've tried to keep it to myself, not sure how it will affect the others. Am I worrying for no reason? There's no proof that anything out of the ordinary is happening, only the feeling in my gut. But is it enough to disrupt final preparations to what we all hope will be a record breaking year?

I'm not sure what to do, and without my darling wife by my side, may her soul rest in peace, I'm not sure what I can *do. I can't disappoint the millions of children around the world, many who will never see a new toy or article of clothing at any other time. I can't let my own feelings interfere with what I know is the right choice. I'm going to hold off telling the others, at least until after every last toy has been delivered. Then, hopefully, I'll be able to understand what's causing this feeling. I just hope it's not going to change anything, but, somehow, I think it might.*

SEVERAL MONTHS passed after Clarence had his conversation with Santa. Now he and Marie met where the green sleigh waited patiently to fly once more. Time had flown past and Christmas was just around the corner. Clarence was no closer to figuring Marie out than she was to figuring him out.

Snow fell with determination as the wind blew at moderate speeds. But the added wind couldn't account for the extra chill Marie felt in her bones. "I'm not so sure about this. I'm not chickening out or anything. It's just that it doesn't seem like the right time to be testing my skills," Marie said as she settled into the sleigh. The fur-lined hood protected her from the wind and cold but still she felt chills down her spine. *Something isn't right. I feel too cold inside.* She gripped the reins tightly in her hands. Her shoulder ached from the tension.

"Don't worry; you'll be fine," Clarence encouraged. He could feel that she was more tense than usual, more so than the last time. "The chills won't last. See, the wind's already starting to change."

Marie looked around as if she could see something in the breeze. After another moment of hesitation, she squared her shoulders. She'd tried so hard to ignore all the demons fighting inside for too long. With seemingly new confidence, she whistled out the first signal. *I can't let him see my fear.*

The reindeer pricked up their ears. Dasher pranced back and forth impatiently, or was it because he felt something wrong too? The other reindeer struggled against their harness. Marie whistled the final command. They ran towards the sky, gaining momentum until they were pawing at empty air.

The bluish-white of the Polar Region was soon left hundreds of feet below. The sleigh picked up more speed as Marie gave the harness a prod. The sleigh leaned towards the new direction. In what seemed like mere minutes, they were flying over the low hills of Russia, and then the frozen plains of Siberia. The wind whipped in their faces as they raced past scores of trees. They were soon racing with the wind and keeping pace with the falling snow. Every movement of the reins caused them to go in a different direction and to unknown places of flight. It was almost as if they moved with the speed of thought.

They soared over the white world below and Clarence let out a whoop. He leaned forward, mentally checking over the harness of every reindeer.

Marie's face lit up with a modest delight. She was actually driving a sleigh, without fear of heights or falling. Earlier apprehensions were forgotten in the thrill of accomplishment. But it was short lived.

What am I doing? Maybe I should just tell him everything. But how can I, after everything that's happened? Her nightmares stared her in the face. She tried to hide their shadows in her mind and succeeded. Hiding them let her enjoy the sensation of flying, if only for a little while.

Marie let out a wild yelp of delight, matching Clarence's own. Her stomach didn't even try to rebel as they flew. She was just getting used to the sensation when he changed the tone.

"Now comes the hard part of the venture," he said in a

tone that was far too calm.

"What hard part?" Marie asked, not wanted to trust her ears.

"Landing," he said as her fingers jerked and the sleigh lurched towards the icy plains of the North Pole far below. He noticed she was clinging to the reins to the point that her fingers, had they not been inside her gloves, would have been white. *I sure hope she knows what she's doing, because if she doesn't we're both not going to make it.* "Did you read the manual?"

"What manual," she replied with panic in her eyes; her stomach was filled with an erupting volcano of bile. She had to swallow back the need to throw up.

Clarence mentally kicked himself. *What manual? The one I forgot to give you.* He grabbed his side of the sleigh for dear life. He was too busy concentrating on not falling out to reflect on anything else he might have forgotten to teach her. The sleigh went into a steep nose-dive and the two screamed like people on a roller coaster. "Pull up! Pull up!" Clarence shouted. *I will not take over. I am not going to take over!*

Marie couldn't comply. She was paralyzed by fear as she remembered that one moment, of plunging towards the stone-hard surface below. The ground came rushing up at them, at over two hundred miles an hour. She finally managed to break free of the shock by closing her eyes. She tried to sing an old lullaby that had entered her thoughts. As she did, she jerked on the reins with all the strength that remained at her command. The reindeer raced back down to Earth, sending up sprays of powdered snow.

Once the cloven hooves hit the ground, the reindeer slackened their pace. Even after their madcap ride had stopped, Marie and Clarence lay back in the sleigh. They gasped for breath, the wind knocked out of both their lungs.

"Next time you should drive." Marie managed a shaky

laugh.

Clarence let go of the sleigh. A relieved smile spread across his face, the kind he used to use when he knew he'd just escaped some kind of severe punishment. His knuckles were still a pale, chalky white. He had to admit that he'd been scared almost to death. Santa made it look far too easy. He was suddenly very glad he wasn't authorized to do any of the Christmas deliveries.

The beeping of his radio changed everything.

"E-two to C-one! Do you copy? Over."

Clarence shakily pulled out the device and thumbed the transmit button. "C-one here. What's the problem? Over."

Static sounded over the frequency as he released the talk button. He waited almost impatiently for a response, not liking the tone in Dena's voice.

"We have a code seven. Repeat, a code seven. We'll meet in the usual place. Over," Dena's voice crackled.

"I'm on my way. Over and out." The radio gave one last burst of static as Clarence put it back in his pocket. He shook slightly as he stepped down from the running board. He couldn't help but remember a similar set of circumstances several years ago. Those circumstances had led to the death of one of his closest friends. He forced himself to stop trembling once his feet hit the cold ground. He had a job to do right now, and his personal life could not interfere, nor could his growing fear. He'd been trained too well. These feelings had to wait.

He turned to Marie with an unreadable expression. "Take the reindeer back to the stable, then go find Sandra." Without another word, he ran to a side entrance that led to the city, vanishing into the shadows.

Marie watched him leave, whistling a command to the reindeer. They ran to a high dune and disappeared. A growing fear beat against her chest; one she could almost put a name to.

TWELVE

BY THE TIME Marie had gotten the sleigh and reindeer back inside, the North Pole had turned into a busy swarm of bees. Elves were teeming everywhere, almost as if at random, but their faces showed a sense of purpose. Marie tried to find Sandra in the bustle but was headed off by several different security teams before she could get close to her.

In frustration, she turned to go to her own room but stopped abruptly when she saw Clarence with several other elves she knew. They turned down a long hallway she wasn't familiar with. Not stopping to think, she followed them. A few elves ran here and there, but the hall was otherwise empty.

Finally, after what seemed like hours, the elves came to a stop. They entered a room she'd never seen before, closing the door behind them. Marie stared at the window in the heavy wooden door. Only vague shadows could be seen through the bubbly glass. She put her ear to the door, hoping to learn what was going on. She'd never heard of a code seven before.

"Intruder -- great threat. Others may follow. More than -- madman. Santa's instructions -- search every -- assigned to this -- Report -- Find anything. Keep an eye on -- anything, radio--"

Marie could make out nothing more, which frustrated her to no end. There was a strange whirring noise, similar an old generator, humming in the background. It prevented her from hearing all the conversation. She could only make out a few odd snatches of words, which only served to make her even more curious.

CLARENCE CLEARED his throat, addressing the security team who now sat at a long conference table. "We all know that this intruder has created a great threat to this establishment. Our security has been breached more than once, in various areas of our organization. I fear other intruders may follow.

"I have a feeling there may be more to this than just a madman after presents, as we have had to deal with in the past. Per Santa's instructions, Dena and her team will be conducting a level-by-level search. As soon as this meeting is over, you will join your respective teams. You are assigned to this building. Everyone is to report immediately to either myself, Dena, or to Santa, if you find anything."

He glanced at their serious faces. He wasn't sure that he wanted to continue with the briefing, but knew he couldn't let his own feelings get in the way so he plodded on. "I have been assigned to keep an eye on Marie. She should be with Sandra right now. If you need anything, radio me, or send someone to find me. I'll be near Santa's office or on the next floor up."

Clarence walked to the back of the conference room as Dena took over. He almost felt like he was betraying Marie by taking the assignment. But someone had to keep an eye on her since she was still an unknown quotient.

An old heater, one of several that hadn't been replaced earlier, hummed in his ears, drowning out all other sound. He'd wished it hadn't been overlooked when they'd last refurbished. The loud noise cut into his thoughts, not that he could concentrate on what Dena or the others were now discussing anyway.

He replayed the last discussion between himself and Santa through his head. He wondered, and somehow felt, that Marie had something to do with all this. She had to be involved somehow. He didn't exactly want to place his suspicions on her. But something in the back of his mind told him that he'd known something like this would happen. If all this had come about because he'd taken pity on her while she was out there, he would never forgive himself. It didn't matter what his feelings for her were now.

It didn't take long for the conference to end. Chairs scraped against hard tile as elves made ready to leave.

SHADOWS MOVED towards the door from behind the closed door. Marie could see their vague shapes in the glass. Noticing a door across the hall, she ran to it, yanking on the handle. She reasoned that it would not look good to be found eavesdropping. The tumblers inside the mechanism slid into place as her heart raced. She looked over her shoulder and slipped into the darkness beyond the door, closing it softly behind her.

The room was darker than midnight with no moon. She moved farther in, trying to feel with her hands and feet. Halfway in, she stumbled over something that reached almost up to her knees, something that felt like cold metal. Trying to regain her balance, she put out a hand for any support she could find and felt the edge of a table. She grabbed on, her feet kicking up dust, causing her nose to twitch. She tried to hold back the sneeze by bringing a hand up to stifle the sensation. It seemed to work and she let her hand drop with a sigh of relief.

The sneeze broke free with greater force than she'd expected. She stumbled backwards, catching her leg on the thing she'd tripped over only seconds before. As she lost her grip on the table, her body slammed into a stack of boxes, tilting them towards her. The boxes slid over each other, trying to reach stability, along with the table's piled up contents.

She threw her hands out to try and stop the avalanche, diverting what she could. The rest of the boxes rattled down around her. One large box tumbled down the length of her body, stopping to rest beside her bruised head. The resulting dust cloud hung thick in the air. A few more boxes rolled over, completely hiding her unconscious form.

SANTA SAT at his desk, looking over yesterday's reports. The curtains in the window swayed, his papers flying off the desk from a sudden breeze. He closed the window with a resounding snap. A sudden prickle went down his spine. He turned, seeing a flash of color out of the corner of his eye as the lights went out. His flesh bristled all over with goose bumps and he looked around, trying to see through the darkness. "Who's there? Clarence is that you? Show yourself now or---"

The rest of the sentence was cut off as a gloved hand forced a gag into Santa's mouth. Strong arms grabbed him from behind. Before he knew what had happened, his hands were bound behind him.

"Walk, and don't try anything," a rough, masculine voice hissed in his ear.

Santa didn't recognize the voice and struggled to get free. The intruder dragged him to a hidden doorway, the same one he'd used to enter the room. He had to pause under the strain of the older man's weight. Santa took that moment to kick over a chair, pretending to trip. He hoped someone in the hallway outside would be able to hear it.

Perhaps sensing that the noise would alert someone from the other room, the intruder pulled Santa through the secret door in a hurry. The panel settled seamlessly back into the wall.

Clarence opened the door to the conference room, holding it open for everyone else. He waited while Dena headed out to begin her search. He was about to follow her but stopped. He turned to the door across the hall. He thought he'd heard something coming from that direction. Several security personal followed him as he went over to investigate.

"I'll be just a moment," he said in response to their unspoken question. "I want to check something out." He tried the knob but it was locked, just like it should be. Just to be safe, he fumbled with a circle of keys until one fit into the hole, the handle turning easily in his hand.

Clarence switched on the light, illuminating old furniture and boxes that were strewn everywhere. Large pieces of canvas hung at rakish angles on strange looking shapes. Dust hung in the air and played tag with the light that spilled into the room. Other than that, the room seemed empty.

He scratched his head. Several boxes had fallen over. They must have settled oddly. No one could have disturbed them. The door to this room was always locked, and only three people had the key.

His companions looked around curiously. There were hundreds of places in here that an intruder could hide in, if they had gotten in. Overlapping tables and chairs formed secret caves. Empty spaces could be found anywhere if one really looked. The whole room would have to be cleared out to find anything.

Clarence stood still, thinking. He looked at a large lump of iron in the middle of the room, scrap metal that someone couldn't stand to have thrown out. There wasn't any dust on the thing. He looked around at the other odd pieces of overturned chairs and tables. Most of the fallen boxes were on the far side of the iron mass. He walked over to them. They had fallen recently, he noted, their dust disturbed and still lingering in the air above them.

"Remind me to look through this later," he said to no one in particular as he closed and locked the door behind them. A sudden burst of static sounded from his radio, demanding attention. He reached for it as his heart began pounding.

"Code Eleven. Repeat, this is a Code eleven. Emergency on 3rd floor. C team report immediately."

"We're coming," Clarence called into the radio. A code eleven was something he'd never heard used before, even though he knew what it meant. It was not good. "This is a Delta Gamma maneuver. Everyone, move!" His team dispersed, running to their pre-assigned stations.

CLARENCE RAN through the halls. He hadn't taken time for even a proper breath after instructing his team before bursting into action. His mind was racing, racing faster than those who followed behind him. He clutched at one side, a stitch forming, but he didn't stop. Up stairs, down corridors, he wondered who had designed this building. He wished he could give that person a piece of his mind, or maybe a kick to the head.

Inside, he kept hearing the message, over and over again. *"Code Eleven. Code Eleven."* A Code Eleven was a high security breech. He didn't even want to contemplate what it meant. His heart was full of misgivings. The incident he kept having nightmares about jumped back into his immediate thoughts. Things had gone from bad to worse during that incident. He hoped that would not be the case this time. All the same, it was hard to not look back and remember.

The H.O. still wasn't sure why he felt that something was off. Perhaps it had been because of how Santa had acted, almost relieved, after his safe arrival back at the North Pole. It had been a record-breaking year, great news to everyone who had worked so hard to make it happen.

Clarence moved towards the ground level of the Main Office

Complex with extreme caution. His heart pounded as he went up the stairs to the third floor. He almost stopped breathing as he entered that office, seeing the signs and knowing what they meant. Without stopping to call for backup, or even to think, he was racing back the way he'd come, hoping against all hope that he wasn't too late.

With some effort, Clarence pushed the thoughts aside as he rushed through Santa's open office door. He stopped cold. His whole body tingled with adrenaline and shock.

Sandra looked at him with sad eyes as he swept a quick glance around the room. Papers were strewn all over. Some of the furniture looked like it had been shoved around in a struggle. It was almost exactly like that last time. "What happened?"

Dena stood up from the desk where she'd been sitting, trying to recreate the struggle in her mind. "I hate to be the bearer of bad news, Clarence, but you might want to sit down for this one. I'm sure you've already guessed what's happened so I'll cut to the chase. Santa's been kidnapped."

Clarence fell into the nearest chair with an expression of disbelief and shock. He ran a hand over his eyes, a headache forming behind them. Images from a similar night ran through his head and he wondered if there was anything that could have been done to prevent it. History wasn't supposed to repeat itself, not like this.

"It's true," Sandra confirmed. "I went down to the Kitchen to get Santa something to eat. I couldn't have been gone for more than five minutes, but when I came back, Santa was gone. I heard a loud noise just after I'd climbed the stairs and came to investigate. I couldn't have been thirty seconds behind them but all I found was this." She indicated the mess around them.

Clarence shook his head. "I don't believe it. I can't believe it. Christmas is only five days away and you're telling me that Santa's missing?" He blinked back the moisture in his eyes, unsure if it was from anger, frustration, or something else.

Dena nodded. "Sandra triggered the alarm, and one of my teams responded. By the look of things, I'm guessing Santa must have put up quite a struggle. We've already canvassed the place and sent anything down that might have fingerprints. I hate to admit it, but whoever did this had to have had someone on the inside. That, or it was someone who knew what they were doing. Which means they'd have to have some kind of knowledge of this place, or an accomplice who did."

Clarence closed his eyes, his heart sinking deeper. "What do we know about the kidnapper?" His voice was calm, expression schooled, as he looked back up into Dena's eyes.

The security chief shook her head. "Not much. Santa never allowed security cameras in his personal space. You know that. I can tell you that whoever it was had to be strong and pretty determined. Since Santa was about five foot seven, I'm guessing that the kidnapper was probably a little taller."

"But it's nothing more than a guess?" Clarence sighed deeply when she nodded. Thoughts of the intrusion in Texas filled his mind, the technician's report that the person seen had to be close to six feet tall. Was there a connection? He didn't like the odds. "What are our options?"

Dena shook her head. "I'm not sure. But, whatever we do, we need to do it fast. And it would be wise to have a backup plan in case things don't clear up."

"You're right," Clarence agreed. He turned to Sandra. "Where's Marie?

Sandra looked up from shuffling some scattered papers. "The last time I saw her was near the Old Corridor. I was going to escort her to her room, just like you'd asked, but I lost sight of her in the crowd. I'm not even sure if she saw me in all the chaos, then Santa called for me. I had to leave and hope for the best."

"And you haven't seen her since?" He shook his head

in disbelief. His original fears were apparently coming true. "This, of all things, had to happen, and at a critical point too." *If she's involved in this, I will never forgive myself.*

Dena tapped the top of the desk. One. Two. Three taps. "We all know that Marie is the only one authorized to take Santa's place. He would have us find her first," she answered. "I can't believe she'd be a part of any of this. She's definitely not strong enough or big enough to force Santa to do anything. Her contact with the outside world has been near non-existent. There's no way she could have called someone in to do it. We've kept careful track of all outgoing communications."

Clarence didn't know if she was saying that for his benefit or for truth's sake, but appreciated it all the same. "When Sandra initiated the intruder alert, you had all public transportation shut down, right?"

Dena wasn't entirely sure where he was going with this but nodded. "It's standard procedure. Only someone with the right access codes can operate the larger scale transports, such as the Subway. And there would be a record of it. The only other known ways out are the usual exits to the surface. I suppose it's possible for someone to walk along the Subway lines. We haven't had any flyovers within the past week, at least nothing within a range of concern. Nothing that could do the kind of touch and go required for an evacuation of any kind."

Clarence rubbed his neck. "So, if Marie, or whoever kidnapped Santa, wanted to leave, they would have a hard time doing that. Unless there was some secret passageway we don't know about. It would be safe to say that they are both still nearby. That being said, we should probably focus our search within the city." He hoped beyond anything that Marie and the intruder were not the same person, or working together.

Dena nodded. "I'll get my teams on it. I'm sure we'll find one or the other before the day is done. Hopefully both."

THIRTEEN

MARIE GROANED. HER head ached and she felt like she'd been pummeled. She tried to roll over and winced. The sensation reminded her of... No, she wouldn't think about that. At least this time she hadn't been falling, a small boon to how she really felt. She tried to move again and managed to dislodge several boxes. The light overhead shone through the opening created from the resulting box movement. She had to squint at the sudden glare; sure it hadn't been on earlier. It took some effort to move out from under the rest of the boxes, and her limbs felt like jello once she was done.

Sitting up, Marie took a quick inventory. Her ribs hurt. Her head hurt. She could feel several deep bruises forming up and down her arms and legs, and wished her head would stop spinning.

After waiting for a few minutes, she tried to stand. Her legs wobbled like soft rubber and she had to put out a hand for support. She didn't think anything was broken and felt glad for that small favor, but her legs folded up under her and she went down. Her vision swam and she blacked out.

It looked like an army had taken over the Main Rotunda, Clarence thought. Every millimeter of it. Several command posts had been set up around the circle. Elves moved to and from various stations. Some were on radios; others were carrying maps and other messages. Clarence watched their activity from the balcony overlooking the rotunda, three stories up. Behind him lay the open door to Santa's office.

"They've moved the security teams into place. And everyone else is out of sight and sound throughout the city," Sandra reported. "No one has seen Marie yet. Dena is worried." She laid a hand on his shoulder. "It's not like her to be gone for so long. Dena reports that she wasn't at any of her known haunts."

Clarence pounded his fist against the railing. "In another four hours, there will be only four days left until delivery time. I don't blame her for being worried." His brows furrowed in deep lines as he went into the office and sat down in Santa's wing-backed chair. The desk reached up almost to his chest from his reclining position. He hit it with a clenched fist, seething inside, angry with himself and with her.

The thought of taking the sleigh out himself crossed his mind. He quickly banished it. Even though he knew how to fly the sleigh, he did not know how to use bag. There was no way he could do it without either Santa or Marie present. He certainly hoped it would not be necessary to find out.

"Clarence?" Sandra followed him inside. She wasn't sure if she should interrupt his thoughts or just wait until he calmed down.

The H.O. looked into her eyes. "Why did this have to happen, now of all times? Better yet, where is Marie when I could really use her help? If she's involved..."

"She can't be," Sandra tried to reason. "Santa wouldn't have trusted her if she was."

Clarence sighed. "Even he makes mistakes. And I don't

want to do the same. I can't decide this on my own. And unless we figure out what is going on, I'm afraid I might have to do something drastic, like canceling Christmas. It's not something I want to do, but for Santa's sake..."

Sandra took his hand and squeezed it comfortingly. She was all too aware of the deep friendship the two men shared. It was something she would never understand, even though she had once been quite close to Clarence. "Whatever your decision is, you know I'll support you. But you have to make a decision. And with Marie not here, there isn't much that you can do. You know Dena will also support you."

"I know." Clarence stared resolutely at the far wall. "I know what I have to do; I just wish I didn't have to do it. I can't help but think of the children. This will break their hearts. I just can't risk history repeating itself anymore than it already has."

Sandra gave his hand one more squeeze before letting go. "Sometimes you have to do what you have to, whether it hurts a few or not. This could be a lot bigger than just Christmas, Clarence. Think outside the box."

Clarence nodded, wincing inside. "Maybe you're right. Tell everyone there will be a meet in the Assembly Hall Thursday afternoon. That gives us a few days. If we haven't figured out what's going on by then, I will have something to announce. I'm pretty sure that few will like it, though." He stood and started for the door.

"Where are you going?" Sandra started after him but stopped when he waved her off.

"I have to do some thinking. Don't worry. I won't disappear." *Not like Marie.*

MARIE STAGGERED towards the Main Rotunda. Pausing, she pressed one hand against the wall for support. She barely recognized the hallway she'd chased Clarence down less than twenty-four hours ago. Her head really ached now and she found it hard to not slump over and fall asleep. She wanted to so badly, but the thought of Christmas Eve looming ever closer told her that she couldn't. Maybe Santa needed her help. Maybe even Clarence needed her, though part of her doubted that. One thing she knew for sure, she needed him.

Her head spun and she thought she heard a voice echo down the long corridor. Thinking about it made her head hurt even more. Someone was definitely yelling at her though. She looked up and saw an elf wavering in the half-light, like some kind of specter. He moved in a sickening fashion and she tried not to faint or throw up, hunching over, eyes wanting to close. "No," she said with cut off breath. "I will not..."

Clarence reached her just in time for her to crumple into his arms. She just lay there so limply against him. "Where have you been? We've been looking all over for you!" He held her up, looking anxiously into her face. He shook her until he noticed her eyes weren't focusing as they should, and that her drooping eyelids were not their usual color. "No, wake up. Don't go to sleep." He noted her pale face, the visible bruises on her arms, the lump on the side of her head.

"I'm so tired, so dizzy. Please, just let me sleep," Marie mumbled as she drooped in his arms, her head lolling to one side. "Let me sleep. I don't care if you lay me against the pipes, uncle. Just don't put me in the water. Anything but in the water."

"All right, I won't." He tried to understand what she was talking about but his concern for her outweighed any curiosity about the water. He rearranged her in his arms so that he could carry her, walking as fast as he dared so as not to jostle her any more than necessary.

Marie groaned in pain. "I promise not to run away again, uncle. I promise. Just don't lock me in the dungeon again. Please, not in the dungeon. Beat me again, but not the dungeon..." her voice trailed off.

Clarence looked down at her with horror. Her eyes

were glazed over. Was she dreaming, hallucinating, or reliving something from the past? He didn't know if he wanted to find out. "Just hang in there. Don't go to sleep. I can't risk letting you sleep if you have a concussion. Try to keep your eyes open for five more minutes. We're almost to Rachel. Just five more minutes." His heart pounded as he said a silent prayer, trying to carry her quickly but gently. He reached the medical department the moment her eyelids could no longer stay open.

Surprised when he burst into the main suite, Rachel looked up from her desk full of paperwork. Instantly, she sprang into action, calling over an assistant to relieve him of his fragile burden. She motioned him to sit down on a low couch. It was obvious that he was exhausted from worry and lack of sleep. She gave him a cursory once over, her brows furrowed with concern. He looked half dazed. He might even be in shock. She gave him something to help with that, assigning one of her nurses to keep an eye on him. That taken care of, she rushed after the other medic to assess Marie's condition.

CLARENCE'S MIND wandered as he sat in the waiting room, a mug of cocoa, that someone had brought, sat next to him. He had a blanket wrapped around his shoulders. He tried to think about what he had to do, but his thoughts kept drifting back to Marie and the condition in which he'd found her. What had she been talking about? What uncle? And why would he put her in a dungeon, or worse, beat her? What was going on?

She was a confusing entity in his life, more so now than ever. He felt like he'd known her forever, but how could he when she wouldn't tell anyone about her past? He had learned more about that from listening to her mad ramblings on the walk over than from her in waking life.

"And right now it doesn't matter," said a voice in his head.

Yes it does matter! He replied. *I know I can help her if I only knew the problem. Maybe if I could find out from Dena, they've become such close friends. Maybe she knows something that will help. I can't just sit by and watch her tear herself apart because of some unknown thing. I have to help.*

Clarence thought back to the times when it seemed like she about to say something but then had changed her mind. Sometimes she acted strange and was oddly silent. And, sometimes, she appeared to be talking to some invisible person. Perhaps it was that uncle she'd mentioned in her ramblings? Clarence was deeply concerned about this. Sometimes the silence was so thick he felt he could cut it with a knife. Her occasional sarcasm did not help either. *I will not give up on her.*

He would not imagine any kind of trouble she might be in. Not now. Not after this. He decided he'd ask Dena about the strange behavior the next time he saw her. He hoped she would be able to shed some light on this mystery for him. With these thoughts swirling around, he finally drifted into a dreamless sleep.

FOURTEEN

SANTA WAS WOKEN by the sound of water dripping into a puddle of water on the floor. He opened his eyes to see multicolored pipes protruding from the far wall; a rusty green one was leaking. The water plinked down into the slowly growing pool, just one-foot below the pipe. Every time the drops hit, they splattered. It caused a unique sound, similar to a dampened marimba or wooden xylophone placed on a cracked cement floor.

There were other things in the room besides the metal pipes. Some tattered fabric lay in a corner. It might have once been some kind of bed. A few empty, overturned crates littered the other areas. The floor and walls were made of crumbling cement. A rusty iron door sat in the far wall. It was locked with a protruding slide bolt. The bolt was so rusted; it was a wonder that it still worked.

Behind the pipes, there was a sizable gap where a hole had been roughly scraped into the wall. It looked as though a desperate person had made it, tirelessly working away at the rotting walls. Dark stains lined the jagged cement. No wonder he'd been tied, not that he could have fit through that hole anyway. Maybe someone as small as Marie might have been able to do so, but he definitely couldn't. Not with his girth.

The Head Elf struggled with his bonds, the gag cutting into the corners of his mouth. The ropes securing his wrists and ankles bit into his old flesh, causing painful welts. He leaned against the wall closest to him, facing the dense barrier of multicolored pipes. He wondered who had made the hole.

There had to be another way out, but the ropes kept him from moving too far. The weak light showed only shadows to his old eyes. He leaned his head back against the wall, eyes closed as he fell into another uneasy sleep.

MARIE LOOKED up at Clarence's face, somewhat gratified to see him worried about her. She'd been dismissed from the Medical Department with what she called "a few scratches" and a mild concussion. Now she was lying in bed, her pajamas covered by her quilt. She didn't know if she should feel more amused, flattered, or simply impatient at his tone. The message he had just delivered certainly wasn't what she'd wanted to hear, but instead of getting upset, she smiled.

Clarence stared at her face, knowing the smile was a front to hide pain, anguish, and disappointment. He'd told her she wouldn't be able to fly the sleigh in her present condition, even though she was in better shape than he'd dared hope. "It's for your own good. You might become more seriously injured and we can't take that chance. You matter too much to be treated like some disposable commodity."

She gave him a funny look. "Why the sudden concern? What about the millions of children out there who are counting on me? We can't cancel Christmas just because I have a scratch. Don't tell me you haven't thought about doing just that. If Santa were here, he'd let me go."

Clarence let out his breath, holding back his frustration. "Well, Santa isn't here. That's the point. If he was here, we wouldn't be in this mess. But since he's not, I'm in charge right now." He turned away so he needn't see the accusing look in her eyes. He'd refrained from threatening to make the deliveries himself, knowing it would only aggravate her, something that would have made Rachel have kittens.

"*We're* in charge," Marie corrected. "We're equal in authority. Santa said so when he made me his Emergency Replacement Specialist. Don't try to boss me around. This has to be a joint decision. You can't go over me. Besides, no one has called a meeting of the Council. There has to be a deciding vote."

"Look!" He whirled around. "I don't care if he made you Man on the Moon, you're not going! And that is final. I won't hear any more arguments. You're not thinking clearly and need to rest."

Her eyes went wide. "Look who's talking. You look like death frozen over. You need sleep just as badly as I do. Aside from which, when I joined the Elf League, I took an oath to serve my fellow elves and humans alike. My life isn't worth anything if I break my oath by not doing my duty as an elf. You wouldn't do that to me, would you?" Marie stared at him with pleading eyes. "I will do all I can to uplift those around me, to serve others before self, to contribute to the greater good."

Clarence shook his head. "The answer is still no. Your oath doesn't count when you're injured and unable to fulfill your duties because of that injury. I took the same oath, remember? You can't go. I'm not going to repeat myself."

Marie folded her arms in frustration. "You're not the boss."

A knock on the door interrupted their debate just as Clarence was ready to throw out another retort. Dena poked her head through the doorway. "Clarence, I think you should see this." She held out a wrinkled piece of paper. "I found this outside Santa's door. Someone inadvertently swept it under the rug." She waited a respectful distance while he read the note.

"To all the elves and humans who work with Santa Claus and his demented crew," Clarence read aloud, "I've decided to shut you down. You've hurt me more over the past years than is worth letting you continue with your stupid charade. So, unless you want us to hurt your "Head Elf", I suggest you cancel Christmas. For good. This is your only warning."

Clarence read the note again. Now he definitely could not let Marie take the sleigh. Not only would it endanger her life, but Santa's too. He had no choice; he had to cancel Christmas.

"I have to go," he said before Marie could utter a word. "There are some things I need to take care of before anything else happens." He didn't wait for a reply before leaving the room, not even bothering to close the door behind him.

"This can't be happening," Marie complained as she reached for her robe, pushing the quilt aside.

Dena hadn't moved but watched Marie as she threw on her robe. "I'm not sure what you're planning, but I'm pretty sure Clarence isn't the only who will disapprove." She walked over to the bed and put a hand on Marie's shoulder. "He's right. You need to rest."

"Don't even mention his name to me right now." Marie removed Dena's hand and headed for the dresser. "I'm not a baby, yet he treats me like a fragile egg. He won't even let me set a foot out of my room. He acts like he's my father and he has no right. My father is dead, and even if he were alive and here in this room, I know he wouldn't stop me."

Dena sat on the edge of the bed and watched Marie pull out a pair of pants. "Don't be too hard on him. Clarence has a tendency to be over protective of anyone he cares about. He really doesn't like it when people get hurt. He's as hard as nails on the outside, but somewhere inside is a heart that's as soft as a powder puff. He just doesn't want to see you hurt more than you can handle."

Marie rolled her eyes. "I'm not a child, not that I know

exactly how old I am, but I know I can't be any younger than he is. I can take care of myself. Besides, I hate to just sit around and do nothing. It's not like it takes a lot to drive the sleigh and go down chimneys, once you've learned how."

Dena took on a serious tone. "I'm sure you've already guessed, but that letter was from Santa's kidnappers. If we try to make even one delivery, I believe they really will kill him. I know Clarence has decided to cancel Christmas deliveries because of that possibility. Santa is his closest friend after all."

"But we can't let him do that," Marie exclaimed as she stumbled towards the bathroom, pulling on clothing as she went. "Think of the children! Can't you talk some sense into him?"

Dena shook her head, aware that the other elf couldn't see her from inside the smaller room. "Once he's made up his mind it's difficult to get him to change it. Besides, what about Santa? Those people aren't playing around and Clarence knows it. He won't dare do anything that could get anyone else hurt."

Marie reentered the bedroom, brushing her hair, gingerly running the brush over the sore spots. "But he'll hurt even more people by canceling. It's not fair to the children. Can't he see that? I know my own limitations, even if he doesn't."

She glanced at the clock, a plan forming in the back of her mind. "There are only thirty hours left, right?" Dena nodded. "We may just have to take matters into our own hands, and I think I have an idea on how we can," Marie stated. "Not a good one, mind you, but I think it will work."

"Oh no you don't," Dena objected. "Think about it. You can't take any chances. What will Clarence say? You know he's worried about you too!"

Marie just stared at her. "Forget Clarence. He won't find out unless you tell him. Besides, he doesn't have to know about it. It's not just Santa we're trying to save, but the whole ideal of Christmas. I know that waking up to find less than the usual amount of presents under the tree isn't a good enough reason to make him change his mind. And if it were just that, I wouldn't do it. But this is bigger than just us, or even the children. This is about everything that holds us together. This is about the most magical time of the year. Please let me do this," she pleaded. "I'll tell you all you need to know about my past. Isn't that incentive enough?"

Dena shook her head slowly, a hint of admiration in her eyes. "This had better be good, or you'll never live it down. I can't claim I'll go along with all this, but I'm at least willing to listen."

Marie acknowledged her friend's willingness. "I'll take whatever I can get, though I'm pretty sure once you've heard my story you'll want to do more than just listen. I'm not going to repeat this, in case someone tries to listen in, so please don't interrupt or it will take forever," Marie warned. "I don't want any more people to know than is absolutely necessary."

"Alright," Dena agreed. "But you drive a hard bargain."

Marie smiled. "I know." She paused, hesitating, then decided to just delve into the most important parts. She was determined to leave out the more painful ones. Dena didn't need to know about those just yet. "I believe I know who the intruder was and if it is the man I'm thinking of, his name is…"

The conversation died down to whispers as Marie finally let out bits and pieces of her past. She hoped the end result would make it all worth living through the nightmare again. More than anything, though, she hoped her plan would actually work. That familiar cold chill returned, even though she knew she was safe with Dena.

THE LARGE grandfather clock in the Main Rotunda struck the hour. The gears counted down the seconds left until Christmas Eve. All the elves sat in the main assembly hall, waiting for Clarence's announcement. Marie twisted her fingers together, heart hammering next to her collarbones. She looked up when Dena took a seat by her. A murmur of voices passed through the crowd. They all knew what had happened, though most didn't know about the threatening note the kidnapper had left. They could only speculate on what Clarence would do about the situation.

Clarence entered from a side door, every voice stopping the moment he entered. He walked over to the podium with a determined air, his face a grim mask to hide the emotions underneath.

"Fellow elves, a most disturbing thing has happened, which I'm sure we all know about," he began. "You are all aware of the kidnapping of Santa. Now Santa's captors have issued a warning that if we do anything, they will harm Santa. With this, and other matters on my mind, it seems the best prospect to cancel Christmas, possibly forever."

Various elves cried out in disbelief as they turned to their neighbors. Their voices subsided as Clarence waved for attention. "I know this may have come as a shock to many of you, but believe me when I say I have looked at this situation from all possible angles. I just can't see how we'll manage to pull the wool over these..." he paused, looking for the most deprecating word possible. "These miscreants' eyes. I know that Santa means a lot to everyone here and I don't want to see him harmed. I am truly sorry to those who had high hopes of a record breaking year."

He didn't wait for comments and left the room directly, before he could change his mind. A murmur of disbelief rose behind him. He didn't want to have them ask any questions he couldn't answer. Many such questions were likely the same he was posing to himself, questions he had no answer for.

Marie looked around the room, only half paying attention to the voices around her. She could understand the disbelief, and even anger, she saw in many of the faces around her. She'd felt much the same way when Clarence had sprung the news on her, but knew there was a way around this. All she had to do was put into place the plan, even if it meant that she would be more in the public light than usual. It was a daunting thought, and she wasn't entirely sure, now that the moment had come, that she was up to the task.

"You're sure you want to go through with this," Dena asked, whispering in her ear. "You won't be able to hide your past for much longer after this. I can smooth things over for now, with hints of new Intel received, but the truth will come out."

Marie closed pained eyes, remembering all the torment and anguish that had brought her to this point. After another moment, she nodded, the decision made. "It has to be done. I can't hide behind a mask of fear. They have a right to know what they're up against."

Dena smiled grimly and stood to walk up to the podium, calling for order. The elves returned to their seats, their voices subsiding as they recognized the Head of the Security League.

"My fellow elves, due to the recent developments, Clarence has cancelled all Christmas deliveries. But," and she held up a hand for silence, "I have received some new information that changes all that. I ask that you please listen carefully. We don't have a lot of time."

ELVES RUSHED everywhere. They talked in hushed whispers as they went about their various tasks. Many scurried like roaches in the light any time Clarence or Sandra came near them. Clarence could only assume they were storing away all the gifts they had made or ordered for that year. Only one thing bothered him. It wasn't that they weren't taking the situation seriously. They were.

Their faces were too grim to give that a second thought. They just acted like they held some great secret. Their expressions were too determined. It was more than a bit unnerving.

He pushed those thoughts aside when the security teams found the trap door the intruder had used. It connected to a tunnel that led to an unused are of the building. From there, another tunnel led to the surface. Somehow, someone had accessed the tunnel to Santa's office, but how, neither Dena nor Clarence was sure. It would not help to follow it now. Chances were good that it would only lead to the tundra, and that their intruder had already vacated the area.

Marie was extremely quiet, but that was to be expected. She didn't try bringing up the deliveries when he visited, for which Clarence was thankful. She'd given him a grim smile that made him feel even guiltier than before. At least she was staying in bed, even if reluctantly. He could tell that she was restless, but refused to let her join him in his rounds.

During his inspections, he watched the grooms carefully. They'd combed the reindeers' coats and hooves to a glossy shine. Other elves shined and cleaned the sleigh. They sharpened the ski-like blades of the runners to perfection, made sure the harnesses were in good repair. The reindeer had to be taken care of after all. The sleigh had to be kept in top-notch condition, if not for the present, for some hopeful future use. Things should not fall into disrepair. Clarence understood that.

The giant fur tree in the Main Rotunda was lit with sparkling lights and decorations. Elves hung tinsel here and there, covering branches with the silvery stuff. They still tried to have a festive air, even though Christmas was canceled. He thought he understood their hidden emotions. Anyone would at least try to keep the Christmas spirit alive, even though it was bound to be less cheery than usual.

Those elves that knew how to sing or play an instrument played Christmas carols. Their melancholy voices made tears come to Clarence's eyes. How could he have canceled Christmas? His heart yearned for a change of mind. His unease grew with every minute.

The elves went about with their usual activities. Many still went around carrying boxes. They never spoke, just listened to the music, looking wistfully towards the upper dome and what lay beyond.

Clarence couldn't take it anymore. He made his way to Santa's quiet office and sat in the big chair where he broke down into silent tears. What had he done? How could he have canceled Christmas? It was about more than just Santa, more than the elves, more than anything else in the world. He put his head on the desk and cried.

SEVERAL HOURS later, Sandra found Clarence still sitting behind Santa's large desk. She touched his shoulder and he looked up, tearstains lining his cheeks. "Only two more hours," she said.

He nodded, heart wanting to cry out in misery. His eyes had a haunted look in them, and not just from lack of sleep. He knew what he had to do but was afraid to speak. Instead, he stood and strode out the door. He couldn't go through with it. He rushed down the hallways, hoping to find the others, to let them know he'd changed his mind.

Holly and mistletoe hung everywhere he went. Candles lit the now empty corridors. There was no sign of any living being anywhere. His heart grew tighter in his chest. He had to hurry before anything else happened. What if the intruder had done more to insure Christmas was canceled? He ran towards the stables, the exact same place he'd run to all those years ago when another intruder had made his way into the North Pole.

Once inside the warm wooden walls, he pulled up short. The sleigh was gone, so were the reindeer. Every hall, room, and corner was empty. Everyone was gone.

Clarence ran all the way back to Marie's room. It was just as empty. He called over the radio but only got back static. All was still. He was deserted on Christmas Eve, the most special and magical night of the year, alone, drowning in his misery and guilt.

SANTA SAT in the dark, also alone, in an unknown place. Christmas Eve didn't feel joyful anymore. His hope of rescue had died out hours before; along with the faith that Clarence would do what he knew was right. He knew that the elf wouldn't be able to abandon his friend, even if it meant doing the unthinkable. Christmas, the way it was known by the children, would die. He knew that it would die.

Clarence, I have watched you for only a short number of years, and yet I feel as if I know your mind. You would never do anything that would hurt me. You always were a softhearted elf. I just wish you could hear me right now.

Don't cancel Christmas just because of me. There will be other Santas, but there will only be one time that Christmas can be canceled and that will be the last. Don't waste it now. I'll be all right. Please don't cancel Christmas when there is even the faintest of hope.

He knew Clarence couldn't hear him, but he could hope that the elf would draw out this wisdom on his own. It was only hope that Santa clung to now.

FIFTEEN

THE NIGHT WAS crisp and cool, with snow falling gently down to earth. A star shone here and there through the clouds. The moon hung like a silver-covered cloud. The wind sang its own carol, the tune slowly gliding over the hills and dunes of snow. Clarence stood there, looking out across the frozen landscape. He thought about the past several months, recalling when he'd first met Marie. Where was she now? He imagined he could smell her soft perfume in the air, a scent like roses and summer. She had brought summer back into his life.

The sound of bells flowed over the world, ice crackling in response. Sleigh tracks lay in the snow in a twenty-foot stretch. Clarence thought he heard the bells just above him and looked up. The sky was empty.

"Clarence." The soft voice echoed in his ears, but it was not the one he'd been hoping for. "Clarence, why are you out here? The temperature's below freezing." Sandra's footsteps crunched in the snow as she joined him.

Clarence turned to face her, head downcast. "They're gone Sandra. And it's all my fault." His voice was hollow. "I just wish it hadn't come to this, though, I suppose I should have expected it."

Sandra moved closer. "You did what you had to. Don't blame yourself for what the others have done. If they want to abandon you, then that's their problem. You don't need them. You never needed anyone before."

Clarence shook his head. "No, you're wrong. Marie was right. I shouldn't have canceled Christmas. Now they're gone and it's all my fault." He clenched his fists. "Why? Why! There were other ways. Something could have been done."

Sandra almost hugged him but refrained, knowing he wouldn't accept it. They'd been down that road once before, a long time ago. But Clarence couldn't walk it with her anymore. His heart never had belonged to her, and she accepted that. Not even when she'd been the only one there for him when they were younger. But no matter what, she would always be his friend.

The sound of bells flew overhead, waiting. Clarence looked up, and this time he saw it. He didn't know what came first, the sleigh or the elves, but, in the end, the order didn't matter. He was so overcome that all he could do was stand there, his eyes threatening to leak more water. He watched as the sleigh swooped lower, happier than he'd even been to see Marie there, the reins in her hands. She brought the reindeer down with ease.

"So," Marie said, looking a bit smug, "you up to giving them all Christmas?"

Clarence smiled and walked towards the sleigh. "Yes, yes I am. Let's give them all Christmas." He climbed into the sleigh beside her, an almost mischievous smile on his face.

Sandra waved as the sleigh began to move off. There wasn't much she could do but wish them luck. She was sure there would be more than enough things for her to do back in the City. Turning away from the disappearing couple, she went in search of Dena.

It was time for the final stage of the plan, the plan that would save everything. No one could cancel Christmas or make it go away, no matter how hard they tried. So long as someone out there remembered the true meaning of the season, it would live on. Tonight, both she Clarence had been reminded of that reason, and it was a good feeling.

THE STARS twinkled above them as they flew over the wooded regions of Germany. The trees were so dark and green in the moonlight. It almost took Clarence's breath away. "What's the time?" He leaned forward to take a closer look at the scenery far below.

"It's 9:30 local time," Marie replied as she nudged the reins.

Clarence glanced over, surprised at how calm she was, even after everything that had happened. He was so relieved to learn that she wasn't involved in the recent tragedies that he felt different somehow. It was like a weight had been lifted from his chest. In fact, he felt rather light and giddy. "Can't you fly this thing any faster," he teased.

Marie smiled and prodded the harness. "If you don't mind going over the speed limit by about fifty times, I wouldn't mind." She thought he looked almost handsome when he smiled.

Clarence laughed but Marie turned her face. He noticed, but didn't comment, feeling that things had somehow changed between them. She was much more confident. He detected no trace of fear in her and he marveled at it. He almost thought he caught a hint of a twinkle in her eye when she'd turned her face, or maybe a faint blush. She looked lovely in moonlight.

"So, what made you change your mind," Marie asked, breaking the silence.

"It was the funniest thing," he admitted, "I just couldn't help but think about what you'd said. And then, with the other elves going around like they did, I began to realize I couldn't really cancel Christmas. It's not something anyone can do. Not alone. It would take the entire world to do that."

Marie nodded. "I could have told you that. In fact, I think I did. Only when people no longer believe can it be destroyed forever. It isn't the presents, or even Santa, that makes it what it is. It's more than that. Much more than that."

Clarence looked at her with an expression she couldn't fathom. These were concepts he'd struggled with for a long time. Now that she'd expressed them, he knew they were true. "You're an amazing person, you know that?"

Marie blushed. "It takes someone as stubborn as you to bring it out in me. I've been awful to you, though, haven't I? What with this plan and all."

Clarence laughed. "Yes, but I deserved it. I wasn't exactly nice to you either, if you will recall. But as for this being entirely your idea…"

She turned to look at him, her expression sincere. "Honest. It was just me, crazy as it was. If things hadn't gone as well as they had, I'd have gone to Plan B. But Dena felt sure you'd fall for it." The look of mischief in her eyes almost made him sorry he'd asked. Was she teasing him?

"You always have an answer for everything, don't you?" He put up a warning finger. "Don't answer that."

Marie laughed. "You know, I've been thinking," she stated and Clarence groaned. "Stop that," she admonished. "I've been thinking that being an elf isn't that bad. It's like being young forever. Did you realize that? And by the way, tonight's the first time I've ever seen you laugh." *Maybe that old ogre does know how to have fun,* she conceded with a smile.

"Marie," Clarence said while shaking his head, "You're one strange girl. I don't know why I put up with you. In fact, I think I'll just dump you out!" He playfully nudged her.

"Hey! If you push me out, then who's going to drive this thing," she complained. He winked. "Oh no you don't. Just because last time I said 'you drive' doesn't mean I meant it!"

Clarence gave her a wounded look. It was a look so comical it reminded her of a sad puppy. She had to laugh. "Stop it! I'm trying to steer this thing!"

He grinned. "Look, next stop," he diverted.

Marie prodded the harness and the sleigh slowed to land on the roof of the first house. She reached for the bag of toys at the same time Clarence did.

"Oh no you don't," he admonished. "I'm going to do this." Clarence grabbed the bag from her. "I may have let you drive but I refuse to let you do any of the hard work. This is a man's job."

Marie gave him a dirty look. "Clarence, who's in charge here? Me. I'm the ERS. Not you. Now get out of my way. And don't even try the macho 'I'm a man' routine. Besides, you don't know how to make the bag work, you said so yourself. I had to pry that information out of Santa."

Before he could retort, she pulled the bag away and plunged down the chimney. Soot shot out, landing on Clarence's clothes and face. He shook his head and brushed at the blackened dust. It didn't want to come off. "Fine," he said folding his arms, even though she couldn't see it. "I might as well let you have your way, since you've got it already anyway."

"I knew you'd cave in," came her reply from deep down in the chimney. "You seemed the type who would. Just so you know, I'm delivering all the gifts this year. Thanks for wanting to help though."

Clarence could only imagine the smile on her face. "At least save me some cookies, okay?" Marie only laughed.

IN ANOTHER part of the world, several teams of elves crouched in the shadows, waiting. With little actual cover outside the building, they'd had to wait for full dark. With the moon hidden behind the clouds, it made the world seem somehow much more sinister.

"Sh, quiet everyone," Dena whispered. "Tommy, take

your group to the far side. James, take your team to the east, Sandy, the west. Get into place. We move on my signal."

Crickets chirped a song to the moving shadows, footsteps crackling on dry leaves and gravel. The minutes ticked by at an agonizingly slow pace. Midnight was almost here. Dena glanced at her watch, counting down the seconds. The elves tensed and then Dena gave the signal. They made their move, forcing doors open, and cutting locks.

Within a matter of minutes, they were in the building, leaving teams of two to guard the exits as the others split up. Some agents went looking for any signs of habitation while the main group headed towards the set of stairs described to them. That was where Santa was being held. The elves carefully descended the decaying steps, hardly making a sound. A door waited at the bottom, dented and rusty with age.

One of the elves pulled out a small tool. The lock was cut in less than three seconds, the bolt removed, and the door opened. The hinges groaned in protest. Once inside, the sound of dripping water caught their attention as it echoed in the smaller space. Then they saw him, propped up against a wall.

"Santa?" Dena rushed to the Head Elf's side and worked to untie his hands and feet, removing the gag from his mouth. "Are you alright?"

Santa stirred from his corner, eyes opening. "I think so," he replied groggily, his mouth dry. "None the worse for wear and tear and lack of food." He attempted to stand but had no strength. They had to help him to his feet and support him as they helped him up the stairs, using a bit of magic so that the stairs wouldn't collapse under the added weight.

"Only a few more steps," Dena encouraged. "You can do it, Santa."

After what felt like forever, they made it to the top of

the stairs. They moved away from them until they were an area clear enough to let them all rest. Santa looked like he needed it.

Dena felt a prickle run down the length of her back and turned to look behind them. Somehow, someone had gotten past the other elves. Dena cursed as a man walked out of the shadows. He was holding a semi-automatic handgun in one hand. "Where do you think you're going?"

Everyone turned at the sound of the gruff voice, surprise filling their eyes. "What should we do," Sandra asked. Their group wasn't prepared to fight. That was the other groups' job.

Dena closed her eyes in thought. She tried to recall everything Marie had told her about the man in front of her, never doubting that he was the one they were looking for. "Leave everything to me." She opened her eyes and faced the man, pushing aside any misgivings or other feelings, opting to take the offensive.

"You might as well give up already," she called out. "You're up against an army of elves. You keep up this charade and you're going to get the crap knocked out of you. And I claim the first round."

Sandra nudged her with an elbow, wondering if it really had been wise to join her on this mission. It had been on rather late notice. But she couldn't just stay home and do nothing, not when everyone else was doing something useful. "Dena, what do you think you're doing? You're only going to make him mad," she whispered.

"That's the idea, " the security chief whispered back. "Trust me. I know what I'm doing." She walked towards the stranger, stopping near the end of the shaking gun barrel. *I hope I know what I'm doing.*

"Don't be stupid," she advised. "Just put the gun down. We outnumber you by, well, six to one, unless you count Santa. But if you really want your hide turned into a leather sack, I'm more than happy to oblige."

The man raised the gun and aimed between Dena's

eyes, one finger on the trigger as he thumbed off the safety. "Shut up, punk, or I'll blow your brains to the moon. I mean it. Shut up!"

"Dena," Sandra hissed. "Don't! Have you gone mad? Just what do you think you're doing? This isn't a movie! He really will kill you!"

"You should listen to your friend," the man smirked.

Dena ignored her and stared down the barrel and into the man's eyes. "And what, exactly, will you accomplish by killing me, Damar Dovan, isn't it?" she asked coolly.

Mr. Dovan rocked back on his heels, surprise registering in his eyes. "Who told you my name?" he raised the gun in sudden rage. "Who told you!"

Dena smiled, hiding any misgivings she felt, her voice as cold as glacial ice. "Someone of our mutual acquaintance. Someone you left for dead five years ago. You thought you'd finished the job, but you didn't."

Mr. Dovan's hands started to visibly shake, the gun barrel wavering as his arms dropped down to his sides. The snarl on his face disappeared, replaced with incredulous disbelief. "No, it can't be her. She's dead. I killed her." He backed up a few staggering steps, eyes wide.

Dena filled the remaining steps between them. "She's alive, despite what you did to her. You're no more than a murdering coward."

Mr. Dovan backed up a few more steps. "That's a lie! She's been dead for years. You can't bring someone back from the grave!"

The other elves looked at each other, unsure of what was happening as Dena continued to press forward. "It's the truth. She told me herself."

"Impossible!" he yelled as he raised the gun barrel, his expression turning maniacal.

Dena only had a moment to warn her friends, yelling at them to drop. She mentally kicked herself. She should have made sure Santa had been safely removed from the scene before trying to provoke her target. But there was nothing she could do about it, not now that the man's finger was squeezing the trigger. She did her best to move out of the line of fire. Even with that last second effort, the bullet grazed her arm before slamming into a nearby crate. Instinctively, she knew he was more than ready to fire off another shot. She just hoped the others had done as she'd asked and were moving Santa to safety. Dovan was hers.

With a grunt of pain, Dena regained her footing, one hand clutching her wounded arm, teeth clenched from the pain. "Not impossible. I talked to her only a couple hours ago. And though I'm sure you tried your best, it obviously wasn't good enough."

Mr. Dovan's eyes dilated, the usually white orbs bloodshot in the dim light. "So I tried to kill her," he snarled back. "I would have gotten away with it if you hadn't meddled. I would have gotten away with everything, even with the kidnapping! You just had to get involved, but you'll never find out why I did it!" He let out a high-pitched laugh, waving his gun.

Dena had no idea how many bullets were in the clip but she knew it was always better to assume the worst and hope for the best. Either way, she wasn't about to take any more chances. "Is that a fact," she grunted through the pain. "I look forward to making you tell me everything."

As fast as a cobra strikes, she was next to him, hitting him behind the knees, causing him to go down. "This is for Marie!" She kicked at the gun still in his hand, sending it flying.

Mr. Dovan growled in rage. He rolled until he could get back on his feet. It happened a lot faster than Dena thought possible, given his build and age. But she could tell he was still dangerous, even without a weapon.

They began to slowly circle each other, feinting with a kick here, a punch there, testing each other's weaknesses. He had the advantage of height by well over six inches. She had more agility and proved it by dancing in under his guard, throwing a jab at the soft flesh just below his ribcage. He doubled over momentarily.

He lunged at her, ready to grapple, hoping to ensnare her with his strong arms. She dropped at the last possible moment, shooting a leg out to trip him. Despite the quick movement, he only staggered, using a nearby stack of crates to restore his balance. He pushed the topmost one over, causing a cascade of boxes to fall all around them. Dena's companions moved further back to avoid getting buried.

Dovan's watch grazed Dena's face as he came in for a right hook. She wiped at the resulting trickle of blood on her cheek. Her eyes hardened further as she saw her adversary reach for something in his pocket. She suddenly realized he carried a knife as he pulled out the folded blade, opening it with a flick of his wrist.

Seeing the look in her eyes, and mistaking it for panic, or maybe shock, Mr. Dovan smiled. "You're all pathetic! Every last one of you! You don't deserve to exist!" He lunged for her, thrusting the three-inch blade towards her, using his full reach to his advantage.

Dena wasn't able to dodge in time and felt the knife bite into her flesh. The blade scored her right arm near the shoulder as she tried to pivot out of the way, using the back of her hand to push his arm away. Almost as if in an expertly choreographed dance, she twisted around his side, her elbow driving into his kidney. Then, using her momentum and already half crouched position to her advantage. She rotated her hips. Her left leg flew up and out, almost as if trying to kick a second opponent in the side. She continued the rotation by whipping her right leg backwards towards her target.

A heavy leather boot made contact with the back of Dovan's head as Dena completed the rotation of hips. Her entire body twisted midair in a surprisingly quick flash of energy, only to land a few feet away from the downed man. One hand rested on the ground, making her look like a deadly panther crouching for the kill. "And that was for me," she said, showing the bleeding puncture wound caused by his knife, even though he was now unconscious.

The other elves finally managed to clear a path into the enclosed space where she and Dovan had been fighting. They had to shift several crates in the process. Sandra let out a sigh of relief upon seeing her friend still standing, even if she was slightly hunched over from the strain of her fight. "Sandy has his accomplices in custody," she informed her, giving the security chief a shoulder to lean on should she need it.

Dena breathed heavily as she pushed a strand of hair out of her face. Sweat beaded on her forehead from the exertion, adrenaline still pumping through her veins. "Good. Radio base and tell them the good news. Have someone bring a gurney for our friend here," she indicated Mr. Dovan with a quick kick to his foot that jostled his leg. "And tell the Kitchen that I'm going to need a really, really big mug of hot cocoa when we get back."

Sandra quickly moved closer as her friend slumped to one side in exhaustion. She signaled for help from one of the other nearby elves who happened to be a field medic. Together they bound the security chief's wounds, then helped her back to the rendezvous point. They assigned the best agents to guard their prisoners, especially Mr. Dovan, even though he was still out cold.

SIXTEEN

THE TOWER CLOCK struck the hour. Soon millions of children would rush to their Christmas trees to see a miniature toy land. They would run and shout for joy when the gifts had all been unwrapped. Small voices would fill the air with laughter. Sleds would be brought out, and races would be won. They would never know what had almost happened. Nor would they realize what had happened to make sure the holiday tradition of Santa would continue.

In another part of the world, elves walked the hallways of North Pole City; sleep in their eyes and contentment on their faces. They traced familiar steps to their beds. Others forged paths to their stations. The year was just starting over for them, even though the New Year had not really begun. Clean up crews swept up leftover tinsel and wrapping paper. Candles were put out. The giant Christmas tree still glowed with lights, as it always would.

A small group assembled in a room just off the main security office. They waited for two more people before heading down the hallway leading to the cellblock. They were a quiet group. Each was caught up in his or her own silent contemplations, recollections of the past year, and thoughts of the future.

Clarence sat off by himself, dark circles under his eyes from lack of sleep, which he hoped to remedy soon. There was just one more thing that needed to be taken care of, a few loose ends to be tied up. He glanced around the room, nodding at Sandra when she looked his way.

Dena wore a sling, the other arm only bandaged from the gunshot wound, which had turned out to be a lot less worrisome than the knife slash. The bruises would heal in time, as would the other hurts. Despite the physical discomfort, she wore an expression of relief, mixed with determination. There were still some answers left to be given, and she hoped that they would have them before too much longer.

Rachel stood ready, in case she should be needed. She was more than aware that at least half of the people at this meeting should be resting in the Medical Department. She permitted this arrangement for the closure they all hoped it would bring.

Santa entered the room, escorting Marie, one hand comfortingly around her shoulders. Clarence wished he was the one holding her, though he knew it was probably better that he wasn't.

Dena stood as they entered the small room, looking closely at her friend's reddened eyes. She was comforted by Marie's composure. Perhaps things would go off more smoothly than she'd hope. "Are you ready for this?"

Marie bit her lip, not sure if she was ready, but nodded anyway. She and Santa had just come from Santa's office where they'd had a long talk. She felt better for the talk. But now that it was time to reveal the most sensitive parts of her past, she wasn't sure if she was quite up to the task.

Dena smiled reassuringly. It had been Marie's choice to get this done and over with, and she couldn't fault her for it. "This way," she said as she led the group down the hallway towards the only occupied cell. The lone occupant glared at them as they moved closer. His accomplices had already been shipped out.

Mr. Dovan snorted in disdain, his hands still cuffed. He also wore legs shackles that were connected to the walls by a long chain. Just in case he tried anything, two security elves stood on either side of the cell. Seeing Marie behind Dena and Clarence, he snarled. "So you did survive. I should have known. You're definitely your mother's daughter. It's your fault, you know." He laughed mirthlessly.

Marie started at that statement, anger filling her as she made to leap towards the bars. Santa's gentle hands held her back. "You know nothing about my mother!"

Mr. Dovan chortled. "Keep thinking that. But I know the truth." He winced and put a hand on the tender spot on his head. He didn't have a concussion, just a throbbing headache, and a lot of pain from the kidney shot.

Marie grabbed the bars as if to shake them, unaware of the pressure of hands on her shoulders. "Tell me!"

His eyes gleamed with a cold light as he sneered. "What? Don't remember? Poor little elfling can't even remember her parents, or how they died! Bet you don't remember what happened before that either, do you?"

Marie ground her teeth, knowing he was baiting her and that he knew she was unable to resist rising to the bait. It was because what he'd said was true. She could recall what her parents looked like, and that she had once lived with them. But she could not remember what had become of them, or what had happened before she somehow knew they'd disappeared from her life. It was far too painful to even try.

Mr. Dovan began laughing again. "I can see that you don't, so I'll have to remind you." He lunged forwards, getting as close to Marie as the chains would allow as he also grabbed the bars, cuffs hitting the metal. "I killed them!" He took great pleasure as she let go and took an awkward step back. The look on her face was worth every injury her stupid friend had inflicted on him.

Marie's legs buckled under her. She was grateful for the added support she felt from behind her as Clarence stepped in so that Santa could rest. "No," she whispered, sinking to her knees, still not sure she'd heard correctly. "No."

Mr. Dovan's sadistic smile spread at her denial. He felt a greater sense of triumph, even though his original goal had been thwarted. "Don't you remember, little elf?" He made the term as close to an epithet as possible, smearing it with venom. "I did it right in front of you, just like this." He moved his hands as if holding a gun, eyes excited as he relived the moment. He pretended to pull back the slide, then fire several shots. If he'd been holding a real gun, the imaginary bullets would have gone straight through her heart.

A sob broke free from Marie's constricted throat. "No." She stared ahead, blind to the room around her. Instead, she saw two older looking elves as they knelt on the ground in front of her. They moved as if being brutally punched, only to fall back and lie still on their backs, blank eyes starting upward. She turned to see the man who had done this, eyes as cold as hoarfrost, gun barrel smoking in his hands.

"You do remember." Dovan's voice was cold in her ears, without any kind of compassion. "But you know they only had themselves to blame. I needed them, and they refused. My revenge could not be completed without them."

Clarence was tempted to force his way through the bars and throttle the crazed man. He would have if he hadn't been trying to keep Marie from falling completely to the ground. Her knees had already collapsed under her. He was torn between a desire to harm and a desire to protect and comfort. With these emotions warring inside, he just knelt there, holding Marie by the shoulders as she swayed in his arms. "You! You...!" His grip on Marie's shoulders tightened to the point of leaving marks.

Dena, despite the surprise confession, remained calm. Her arms were folded as best as they could be with the sling in the way. She was well aware of the shocked expressions of her fellow elves. "Revenge for what?"

Damar Dovan snarled at her, turning hate filled eyes in her direction as he released the bars and raised a pointing finger. "For the death of my father! You killed him! All of you! You're all responsible!"

Santa stared wide-eyed at this clearly insane man. The accusation was so unbelievable. He wasn't sure if his shock came from the actual words, or the possibility that it might be true.

Clarence froze in his attempts to comfort Marie. He remembered that one Christmas night. It was something that had happened over five years ago.

Clarence had run towards the nearest trolley station. After he'd seen the disheveled state of the Head Elf's office, and the partial note, he knew exactly where to go. He just hoped against hope that he'd be in time to stop what he knew was going to happen. He urged the driver to speeds beyond the car's design. He didn't even wait for it to slow down once he'd reached his desired destination. All the time, he'd been calling frantically over his radio, hoping that someone was closer. Anyone.

With a stitch in his side, and short of breath, Clarence pushed towards the stables. He was forced to slow down so that he didn't pass out. His breathing came in short gasps. He saw Santa's coat and hat near the entrance of the tunnel used to take the sleigh to the surface. It told him he'd guessed correctly about where the man had gone.

With more effort than he cared to admit, he pushed onward, through the tunnel that led outside, afraid of what he'd see. At the top, he rounded a dune and stopped, hands slowly reaching upward at the scene before him.

"Don't move, or I'll blow his brains out," the haggard man shouted. His crazed eyes held a maniacal light that disconcerted the elf. But what was even more disconcerting was the sight of who was

with this man, the Head Elf, held in a vice-like grip by the psychotic intruder.

Santa looked towards his Head of Operations with pleading eyes, his mouth covered with rough tape. His hands were bound behind him with some kind of cord. A gun was held to his head, though Clarence wasn't sure what kind. He was too shocked to process much of what was happening. He moved a few steps closer, edging out onto the ice, hoping to keep the man from becoming more agitated. "Let's talk about this," he offered, heart hammering against his ribcage. "Maybe we can work something out."

"There's nothing to work out! It's your fault! All your fault!" The man swung his gun wildly to indicate the whole polar region. "It's because of you that I lost everything! My wife! My son! Everything! If it weren't for this place, I'd never have lost everything I loved!"

Clarence tried to reason with him, but realized there was no point. This man had lost all sense of reality, trapped in a mental prison all his own. Not even sure what he was saying, he tried to convince the man further, but knew it was useless. He only hoped there was something he could do to make this deranged man take his life instead, and leave Santa alone. He would do that much for a friend, sacrifice his own life.

Unfortunately, Clarence forgot he'd called for backup. He didn't expect the sudden appearance of more elves. The man's eyes widened at the sight of them entering the wind swept pocket canyon. "I told you not to move!" His gun swung around as he pulled the trigger, sending out what sounded like a sonic boom, which echoed off the ice cliffs around them. The large icicles around them began to shatter and came crashing down. One of the larger chunks fell towards the man and his hostage, crushing both beneath its great weight. Elves scrambled forward to try and break the massive icicle as Clarence ran to Santa's side.

Blood seeped from the older man's mouth as Clarence removed the tape. "Clarence," the Head Elf groaned as ice chips flew from the other elves' efforts. The old man's head rolled to one side and remained still, his chest crushed under the immense weight of the frozen water. The body of the intruder was already losing heat from the intense cold around him, lying lifeless next to the Head Elf.

"David Dovan," Clarence half whispered in shock, realization opening his mind to the similarities between the two incidents. "You're his son. I knew there was something familiar about you. You're the one who's been breaking into all the different way stations. It was you all along."

Damar gave a slight bow. "Of course. After you changed things, I had to find new ways inside. Ways I could have found much more quickly if that one," and he spat at Marie, "had actually done as she was told! "Just get me in, " I said. Just use your precious little elf magic to make it happen! But no, you wouldn't!"

Marie looked up as his tone became more and more agitated. "You used me," she said in a quiet voice, "just like you used my parents. You used us! And for what? Your stupid revenge? Is that what this was all about? All those nights when you locked me up in that dungeon when I wouldn't, or couldn't, do what you wanted me to do? All those times you," she paused, shuddering, "beat me until I couldn't move?"

Clarence rocked back on his heels, more shocked by this new information than he had been by anything else. Several pieces fell into place as he contemplated what they meant. He mentally kicked himself for how he'd treated her all this time; completely unaware of the harsh life she'd led.

Tears were streaming down Marie's face as she stared at the crazed man before her. "And then, when I couldn't take it any more and tried to run away, you tried to get rid of me just like you did my parents! All for what? Because your dad lost it and you couldn't come to terms with that?"

Damar lunged at the bars again, causing them to rattle, cuffs digging into his wrists. Spit flew from his mouth. "I could have gotten away with it too! I could have punished you all for it! If only you'd died like you were supposed to!

It's all your fault! Every last one of you! It's your fault! It's all your fault!"

Something inside of Marie snapped, breaking free from the ice encased fear that had held her back for so long. "My fault?" She got to her feet in one fluid motion, moving closer to the crazed man. Her fists were clenched at her sides, back ramrod straight. Fire smoldered in her eyes, the same kind of fire that she'd focused on Clarence the first time they'd consciously met.

Tears still coursed down her cheeks but now in angry streaks. "My fault?" She let out a mirthless laugh, her voice cold. "No, Damar Dovan. It was your fault, yours alone. I reject your blame. I reject everything you ever claimed to be to me."

Before anyone else could even guess what Marie was doing, she had moved her hands upwards. With her elbows bent, power surged around the clenched fists. "And I reject you!" She opened her hands, pushing her palms forward as her eyes turned an icy blue. A blast of arctic air rushed towards the frothing man, pushing him back against the wall so hard that his head cracked against it.

"And it will be a warm day in the South Pole before I can ever forgive you for what you've done to my family."

Clarence felt like his jaw had come unhinged and was hanging by a single pin as he stared at the woman in front of him. He couldn't believe his eyes as he looked past her to the unconscious form of Damar Dovan. The barest hint of the frigid air that had blasted the mad man still hung in the air, sending tendrils of frost up and down the metal bars.

Without so much as another word, or a backward glance, Marie turned and walked back down the hallway. She didn't look to the left or right until she was back in the open foyer of the Security League's main office. As soon as her feet met the smooth tiled surface, she was running. She ran as away from the staring eyes and the questions that would follow. She knew that she couldn't answer them. Not yet. Maybe not ever.

Sandra moved forward a few steps, not sure what to do after such a commotion. She glanced at Santa, who stood unmoving, a look of shocked contemplation on his face. She wondered if he was having the same problem processing what had just happened that she was.

Rachel moved into Dovan's cell to check for vital signs. She was relieved to find them strong, despite the new sizable lump on the back of the man's head. He would wake with a killer headache, but it would give them plenty of time to move him to a more permanent location. She knew Dena already had a place in mind where he and his henchmen would never trouble anyone again. It was a place that had something to do with polar bears, if she was remembering correctly.

Everyone else moved as if in slow motion, trying to assimilate the raw data flowing sluggishly in their brains. Clarence vainly wondered how and where Marie had learned to use her magic in such a way. He was shocked. Only someone with a strong flow of power could have mustered such a controlled manifestation. She could have just as easily encased them all in ice without meaning to do so.

Santa glanced at his Head of Operations, coming to terms with what he'd just seen. A slight smile tugged at the corners of his worn lips as he watched his friend's expression change to awed admiration. At last, the elf had met his match. He turned with a knowing smile. With hands clasped behind his back, he walked towards his own office, whistling as he went.

TWILIGHT WAS uncommonly clear. The stars winked at each other and Marie exhaled, her breath becoming a fine mist in the cold air. A cool wind teased some loose flakes of snow lying on the ground. It whistled in her pointed ears. The quiet made for a lovely end to such a hard week. She needed that solace to come to terms with her own actions. She hadn't even thought, just acted out of pure instinct. It was entirely possible that she was more shocked at what she'd done than those who had seen it happen.

Marie stood on the top of the world, just looking at the greatness of the universe before her. Above the city, out on the ice, the cool air caressed her pink cheeks. She sighed as a star fell from the sky. Tears welled up and threatened to fall. One lonely drop slid down her cheek and fell to the icy plain below. It froze into a perfect sphere before being buried in the snow.

She watched the graceful swoop of ice crystals that danced around her like a whirlwind. The intricate patterns and turns fascinated her. Her hair was flung around into her face and away, like a billowing cape as the snow lifted from the ground, creating a lacy curtain of white. It wrapped around her, then scattered to places all over the world in trails of childish laughter. The snow rained down smooth flakes as the moon rose in the sky, casting silvery light over the ice canyons around her.

Somewhere, the sun peeked his proud head above the distant hills of the nearest continent. His warm rays fell down to the earth, warming frozen lands far away. There, the skies turned purple, magenta, and then blood red. But the sight of the silver moon reflecting back the deep blue of the glacial ice was more beautiful.

SANTA WATCHED as Marie stood looking out to the sky, aware of the anger and grief she held within. He had felt similar feelings too many times in his own life, before and after he'd lived at the North Pole. He longed to comfort her like he would a child. But when he saw a breeze blow the snow around her like a comforting hug, and then just as quickly, he knew it wasn't necessary.

Clarence watched the scene, his body warring with his mind. He wanted to go to her, but wasn't sure if he should. When the previous Santa had died, he'd wanted nothing but solitude for weeks on end. He supposed her grief was similar to his own, but couldn't be sure. He didn't know if she wanted solitude or the comfort of someone holding her close.

"Go ahead, Clarence. I'm sure she could use some company," Santa gently prodded.

Clarence looked at the Head Elf, questions in his eyes. They were questions he couldn't put to words as he waited for answers he knew he wouldn't get. And yet, to know more about her past, as tragic as it was, would help. At least he hoped it would. But how to ask!

Santa didn't need to look to know the questions in the elf's heart. "She needs time. There are just too many memories to deal with right now. Give her time to find her self again. Let her feel the warmth of the New Year, and renew in its glorious joy. Let her feel the warm embrace of one who cares and understands. And give yourself that time too." *To come to terms with the amazing potential you two have together.*

Clarence blinked in surprise, realizing that the man had guessed at his own personal anguish over past events. He found that he was grateful for it. And just like with Marie, he was far from ready to talk about it. He still felt partially responsible for the last Head Elf's death.

Santa left him where he stood; the air was too cold for his weary bones.

Clarence sighed and walked towards her. The moon seemed to follow his footsteps as he walked, filling the leftover prints with stars.

MARIE LOOKED longingly out to the sky. The moon, though not yet seen from her vantage, was rising. She drew her arms closer around her waist and stared into the crisp winter air, wishing her mother and father could have been there. She had a feeling they'd be proud of her.

Clarence shuffled the snow as he walked over so that she'd know he was there. She turned to him, the tears suddenly falling as if from a floodgate. She fell into his arms and he held her, letting the tears fall, caressing her long, silky hair.

SANTA OBSERVED them from the sleigh tunnel entrance, a few tears leaking from his eyes as he watched. They had come a long way and still had a long way to go, but they would get there. He was sure of that. He silently wished them luck as he made his way back into the warmer air of North Pole City.

APPENDIX

MODES OF TRANSPORTATION

The Subway

The Subway is a transportation system inside a network of underground tunnels that span the entire planet, allowing elves to reach any destination within a matter of only a few hours, pending on the destination. Traveling at speeds only matched by a Blackbird jet, the Subway is the perfect transportation solution for Santa and his busy elves.

The Subway is located several hundred feet underground, lower than the subways found in metropolis areas using underground systems. The system is reached through a complex gateway created to confuse humans and any others unauthorized to use the system.

Each gateway is unique to its location, being cleverly hidden, generally in buildings, human subway stations, or other innocent looking structures. The entrance to each gateway is hidden behind a façade cleverly constructed to imitate the area surrounding the portal. The façade can only be removed by a code of either vocal origins or by a sequence of touched patterns on the façade itself.

Once past the façade, the actual portal gate is revealed. It is a door that appears similar to elevator doors used in almost all multi-story buildings. This door requires only the dexterity needed to press a single button in order to open it. This leads to the heart of the gateway.

This portion of the gateway is called the Lift or "drop", as the elves prefer to call it. There is a slim but well constructed metal railing that surrounds the entire room, which is only five feet in diameter. This railing is bent inward, allowing the individuals in the car to hold onto the rail without having to make contact with the walls of the shaft.

The floor is of a metal mesh similar to those used in steel-framed buildings under construction. A small gate opens and closes to allow individuals inside the car, which sits directly over the "drop" shaft. There is no ceiling to the car.

The car itself is kept from falling by two thick metal prongs that resemble forklift tongs. These prongs rest directly underneath the car, supporting the length of it. Once activated, the prongs drop downward into grooves in the wall. Released, the car will then plummet downward in a controlled free fall.

Inside the car, near the door, or gate, is a control box that controls the prongs. It also activates an electro-magstatic bubble that surrounds the car, creating a sense of artificial gravity inside while allowing the car to descend at what some call terrifying speeds.

The electro-magstatic bubble is a bubble of energy composed of static electricity and magnetic energy and operates on a principle similar to the magnetic forces used in a monorail system. The descent, though basically free fall, is controlled through the use of the magnetic force, either speeding up or slowing down the Lift when properly applied. The ratio of magnetic energy is controlled from the control box. Any individual using the control box must be completely competent in its use and must have passed a competency test in order to use it.

Since not all elves who use the system have passed their competency test, an elf is always stationed near the bottom portion of the gateway and may be summoned to control the car through a small communications unit installed just off of the car control box. A separate control panel is then used from the bottom portion of the gateway. The progress of the car is monitored from below and controlled by the individual in the main gateway area who also controls and monitors the use of the actual subway transports.

The walls of the shaft are lined with stone, which has

been marbled with a metal alloy that contains strong magnetic currents. These currents are controlled through the control box in the car or by use of the control panel in the main gateway.

When not in use, the magnetic energy is allowed to maintain a resting position, being controlled into a horizontal orientation. When in use, the magnetic field is manipulated to send waves to slow the car to resting potential at either the top or bottom of the shaft.

To return the car to the top of the shaft, an opposite charge of magnetic energy is applied, propelling the car upward. The Lift car is constructed of almost the same metal alloy. The electro-magstatic bubble is always active during any transportation of the car and only deactivates once the car has come to a complete and secured stop at either the top or bottom of the shaft.

In emergencies the car can be stopped before reaching either portal and can be suspended in that place for several hours should it be necessary. The direction can also be reversed, mid-drop, if necessary.

Once the car has reached the bottom, it may be exited in the same manner that its occupants entered, by opening the gate attached to the railing and exiting the car. This leads to the main gateway.

The main gateway is also the station, being a large room of crescent or semi-circle shape. The "drop" shaft is in the middle of the crescent. To the left of the shaft is the control station where the control panels are located for the shaft and the actual station. It is here that all incoming transports are monitored and directed.

There is always an attendant present to control and monitor the station. The attendants trade off in shifts, the new attendant usually arriving on one of the transports. It is the responsibility of this individual to keep the system running smoothly, reporting any problems immediately, including any emergencies.

Since there are literally thousands of different junctions

in the subway tunnels, they are also responsible for helping to route the transports or trains through the correct tunnels.

Each attendant acts as a sort of air traffic controller for the transports, directing them through the appropriate tunnels and giving information about detours and other conditions affecting the transports in their area, including general warnings, as well as suspensions of all activity.

On the right side of the shaft can be found the lavatories and maintenance closets, which include first aide kits, and other sanitation products that may be needed in the station for its regular maintenance and cleanliness. The lavatories are separate for male and female.

The rest of the station is comprised of a waiting area where several comfortable chairs have been stationed, and the actual platform where loading and unloading occurs.

The platform is one foot lower than the main room and is reached by a shallow set of stairs or ramp. When a train is boarding there is a noticeable gab of about half a foot between the transport and the platform, which can be eliminated by placing a compact wedge between to create a gap-free space for the loading or unloading of items on trolleys or carts.

Inside the subway train are several rows of padded benches, one row in the back and one at the front, both facing inward, as well as one along the far wall. Across the top of the compartment are several horizontal poles, spaced apart by about one foot, should a passenger prefer to stand. It also creates room for any items that may need to be transported from location to location.

Each transport contains two cars attached end to end, as well as a cabin or cockpit. A driver or navigator is always on duty in the cockpit of each transport in use. Although there is space for two navigators in each cockpit, there is usually only one in attendance, unless deemed necessary by Central Control. The cockpit is open to view from all in the passenger areas.

It is the responsibility of the navigator to control all passengers and items he or she may be transporting, maintaining a safe transport environment for all involved. He or she is also responsible for making sure that the transport arrives at its destination safe and sound and on time. They must control the speed of the transport and, in part, the location of the transport.

The station attendants can't control all lengths of the tunnel system as some are outside their reach. It is then up to the navigators to choose the appropriate tunnels, controlling the magnetic energy used to propel the transports, closing off certain tunnels by changing the current, or opening them by the same method. The attendants inside the gateway stations assist with this process from their respective stations.

The tunnels are lined with the same metal alloy that lines each drop shaft; as such, the same magnetic energy is used throughout the system. Because the energy is a natural extension of the rock quarried to create the tunnels, any unallied individuals or governments cannot easily detect it. This allows the elves to maintain their privacy and secrecy in express transportation.

Each train is made of the same metal used to make the cars from the drop shafts. A similar metal alloy, which is more flexible, allows the transport to almost meld with the surrounds, be it straight tunnel or curved. It is also why the two cars can be melded together without the need of a connecting device.

This alloy is also lightweight, allowing the electro-magstatic bubble used in the drop shaft to be used in the tunnels as well. The static electricity used in the bubble partially suspends the transport in the air while composing a bubble around the train and supplying any needed energy to keep lights and other necessary equipment functioning.

The magnetic field adds to the stability of the lift, similar to how the monorail system used by humans works, also lifting the car from the "rails" in the tunnels. It also adds a greater charge to the bubble surrounding the transport. When the current is switched on, the negative and positive forces of the magnetic energy propel the transport forward. The more concentrated the opposing energy, the faster the transport travels.

The tunnel system is set up in such a way as to allow two separate tracks so that one train can be loading or unloading while another train continues to run without disturbing the stationary one. When coming upon any station, the train navigator is given the option of taking the second track around the station or the track that leads directly into the station. All trains are required to continue along the farther track unless loading or unloading, or in an emergency.

The transports can generally travel around several hundred miles per hour, pending on the schedule of the particular transport, which route is taken, and the navigator in charge of the transport. In emergencies, the transport will travel up to speeds only reached by a Blackbird, but at greater risk.

Though capable of handling high speeds, the transports are not meant to travel for extended periods of time using the excelled speeds sometimes necessary in emergency situations. During such occasions, the metal has been known to conduct extreme amounts of heat, generally compensated for with the electro-magstatic bubble. The navigator may lose control of the transport, resulting in either high compact collisions or fracturing from hull stress. Only certain models are capable of reaching such speeds, minimizing the risk of such an event happening, along with the possible temptation of "hot wheeling".

A regular schedule is maintained for the entire system that all must adhere to, unless previously informed, so that everything runs smoothly.

The Control Center is located inside the city limits of North Pole City where the largest gateway station is located. Since this larger gateway is inside an elf city, the

Lift is not necessary to reach the station. The Control Center is located inside this gateway station, which encompasses several thousand square feet of space, including two stories to house the necessary equipment and personnel to staff the Center.

The Subway, despite its complex system and possible malfunctions, is the safest mode of transportation in use by any civilization. Accidents are very rare and are generally minor.

To insure security, a net of jamming devices that confuse any devices such as human-created sensors, and other related devices, surrounds the tunnel system. Since the tunnels are embedded in firm rock, there is little threat of their being found by echo locators or sonar devices.

Some gateways are found inside way stations, or other instillations meant for elf habitation, including way ports and other storage facilities. When gateways are found inside such structures, they may, or may not, have a drop shaft, pending on the location of the station, as well as the type of facility it is located in. Those that are above ground, or no more than fifty feet below ground, will include a drop shaft. Those instillations that are further underground will have a special, shortened shaft that leads to the gateway.

The Trolley

The Trolley is a transportation system used inside North Pole City. Because the city is rather extensive and vehicles are not used, with the exception of carts and other small transportation systems used for cargo, a transportation system became necessary for the inhabitants. The entire city is laced with the tracks for the old-fashioned trolley system, including the overhead cables to maintain power.

Stations are located at all major junctions of the city for easier loading and unloading of passengers. The trolley never completely stops at any given time, continuously running, even at night for those who may have overnight shifts, or who simply wish to visit the various parts of the city at later hours.

Each trolley station has a set of stairs that lead up to the main platform, which usually is between ten and fifteen feet long. Each station also contains a row of benches for those waiting to board the next trolley, and those who need a place to just sit and relax. The station platforms are level with the floor of the trolley cars so that any individual wishing to enter the trolley may do so by merely walking from the platform directly to the trolley car. The car will slow down during this procedure to insure the fewest amount of accidents possible.

It is necessary that any entering the trolley walk along the length of the platform to gain the same momentum as the trolley. This minimizes any potential jolts received from a sudden change in velocity. Only those on the slightly insane side will attempt to enter the trolley car without walking with it to gain the proper momentum to reduce any discomfort. The usual method is for the passenger to pick a pole on the trolley car to use as a balance, holding onto this pole as they walk with the car until they gain sufficient momentum, or confidence, to enter the car before the platform ends.

The trolley may be exited at any time by simply walking off of a set of steps located on either side at the front and back of the trolley car. It is suggested that any individual disembarking in this manner should walk along with the trolley until they feel comfortable in letting go to maintain their balance and equilibrium.

To exit at a station, one may either walk onto the platform or swing out onto the platform before the car reaches the station. Keeping up a momentum that will sustain equilibrium and reduce the disorientation sometimes caused by a sudden change in velocity is strongly recommended.

A driver, who is always in attendance, controls the velocity of each trolley car. Very rarely must the driver control the actual destination of the trolley, as the tracks dictate a continual course throughout the city. There are always at least ten cars always running at any given time to insure that no elf is left waiting long for the next car.

The Trolley system is not intended for use of transporting items from one location to another and is reserved for the transportation of passengers only.

The Railway and Cart Avenues

The Railway is a system used for the transportation of cargo or freight from one location to another. It is not intended for public transportation, although several attendants are spaced along the train's length to insure proper loading and unloading of cargo.

The Railway, unlike the Trolley system, does not encompass the entire city. Rather, it travels a specific course between the different buildings associated with production and storage, including Wrapping, Import and Export, and the Subway.

The train itself resembles a freight train, except with all open cars, excluding the engine car. It is about two-thirds the size of a normal train and is powered by an advanced energy source not yet harnessed by human technology, which runs more cleanly than any known systems outside of the North Pole Organization.

The Cart Avenues are regularly travel paths used by both carts and sledges to transport lightweight cargo or freight from department to department, or from one location to another. It is not as efficient to use this system when attempting to send large amounts of cargo from one building to another, and is generally used only interdepartmentally or to transport lightweight cargo through the city.

There are no assigned travel paths for the carts and other small transportation means. Such routes have been established more by habit than actual order. This system is also used to transport any mail to and from the different buildings and departments.

DEPARTMENTS AND BUILDINGS IN NORTH POLE CITY

The Main Office Complex

The Main Office Complex (MOC) encompasses a large variety of offices, including Santa's Office, The Head of Operations' (HO) office, several secretary offices, records, the List office, the Kitchen, the Medical Wing, the Main Rotunda, the Security League office, and the Elf League headquarters, as well as various underground passages and rooms. It also contains the quarters of the Head Elf, the HO, and other upper level staff, including the Emergency Replacement Specialist (ERS). The basement level is reserved for storage.

The Main Rotunda, a large open space in the front of the building, encompasses a large area that reaches up to the fourth floor. It encompasses several private recesses for either meditation, small meetings, resting one's feet, or for socializing. At the far end of the room is a rather large fireplace in which at least five full-grown humans could stand with comfort. The fires contained within this hearth are often small, providing a comfortable blaze for any who wish to tarry near its confines.

In the middle of the room, standing about one hundred feet tall, is the Ever lit Christmas tree. It is so tall that it reaches up into the next three levels of the building. The building is constructed so that the middle section is open for the tree to stand unhindered, with the ceiling being domed above it. Each level balcony around the Main Rotunda is ringed with a sturdy railing for safety.

Behind the great fireplace is the main **Kitchen**, sharing warmth from the fires of the grand fireplace to help prepare the various foods served. There are two areas to the Kitchen, the actual kitchen area and the dining area, which can accommodate several hundred elves at any given time. Since most of the elves prefer to eat at either their respective work sites or in the privacy of their own homes, more room is not needed.

To the left of the Kitchen is the main assembly room where the League of Elves meets on a regular basis. Emergency meetings and councils are also housed inside this room.

Like the Main Rotunda, the assembly room consists of three levels, providing seating for tens of thousands. The head of the room contains a platform with podium and seats for the Council of the League, which includes the North Pole Council. All league representatives on the council are voted in by their respective League associates. Various equipment, used for recording the meetings, can be found throughout the room, allowing those who were unable to attend to view the meeting in the privacy of their own homes.

The second level of the Complex houses the various offices and records rooms of all the children around the world, including the List office. This is where the Head Elf's office, as well as the HO's office may be found. The Head Elf's office is in the back of the building and has a balcony view to the outside. The view presented by this vista is as far reaching as it is spectacular.

The third and fourth levels are reserved for the housing of the various upper management, including the Head Elf, whose personal quarters are the largest on the third floor.

The Security League (SL) headquarters can be found to the left of the Main Rotunda on the main floor, almost adjacent to the assembly room but in its own separate wing, which is separated from the rest of the Main Complex by a connecting hallway. Inside SL headquarters is the main office used most often by the Head of that league. It is here that a record of each elf in the North Pole Organization (NPO) is kept, including any criminal histories, as well as information on any humans working inside any NPO controlled areas, or with the NPO on the outside.

Just off of the main office is a similar office where all equipment used for monitoring the areas sensitive to outside influence is kept. Surveillance equipment is used throughout the entire North Pole City as well as the areas above and surrounding it.

Down a short hallway from the main office is a small bank of holding cells for any intruders, or those who break the law. The stay of any detainee is generally of short duration, though each unit provides all necessary effects for sustaining normal life functions, including lavatories.

To the right of the Main Rotunda is the hallway that leads to the Medical Wing (MW). This wing is far more expansive than the Security League headquarters, housing several operating rooms, an emergency room, several treatment rooms, as well as several extended care rooms.

It is in the extended care areas that those who require various levels of care are housed, including long term, crucial care, intensive care, and limited care, each with a specialized team directed by the Head Medic. Each of the different departments of the Medical League shares space in this wing.

An emergency Subway station is located in the basement level of the building.

Security

More often called the Security League, the security department was created more for outside security than for internal security. This "league" is staffed by highly trained individuals and is under the leadership of the League Head, or security chief, who reports directly to Santa. This person also forms the fourth member of the North Pole Council (NPC), with equal authority to the Head of Operations and Emergency Replacement Special, who are second only to Santa Claus.

The main headquarters for the Security League are found in North Pole City, but there are several different local offices scattered around the world. Several precincts patrol the areas surrounding all import and export stations, as well as major drop shafts and other Subway entrances.

It is the job of the Security League to make sure that normal operations are able to proceed according to schedule and without interruption from outside forces. There has been the occasional breach in security by outside forces, but such attempts to infiltrate the North Pole Organization (NPO) were countermanded by members of this league.

The Security League is also charged with the upkeep of harmony in all elf controlled regions, and have been granted full rights in prosecution and containment procedures, should they be necessary. Such uses of the league are often unnecessary, as the majority of the elves prefer to work in harmony to keep the maximum amount of productivity.

The occasion disagreement will break out, often needing assistance to end the disputes. That is when the Security League steps in. All other occurrences of internal security measures relate to making sure that the laws and regulations of the NPO are followed.

The majority of their work is with external security as this is a more pressing matter.

Medical Department

The Medical Department houses the Medical League, which is the collaboration of medical professionals working in and for the NPO. All medically trained individuals are a part of this league. It is their duty to insure the health of all members of the NPO.

Occasional work injuries are sustained and require treatment. The Medical League responds to such occurrences within record time, and generally remedy the situation within several days, depending on the severity of injuries sustained.

Elves, like humans, also contract illnesses, such as Chicken Pox and the Flu. Other more serious illnesses require containment and it is the charge of the Medical League to make sure this containment takes place, quarantining off areas as needed.

The Medical league is controlled by the Head Medic. This individual is usually the most skilled Medic in the league, or the most respected. It is the responsibility of this individual to make sure that all related actions are in accordance with the Hippocratic oath that each member had to take. He or she must also insure the quality of the care provided, as well as make sure everything is kept within the ordinances of the NPO.

There are several departments within the Medical League. The Research department is in charge of the research and development of new medical procedures and medicinal developments. The Practicing Department contains the actual practicing medical professionals who are authorized to make treatments, assess patients, and perform any required operations or other related processes. The Nursing department is comprised of the lower medics who work under the direction of the Practicing Department, aiding in any medical procedures required of them. The final department, but by no means less import, is the department for Safety and Work Med. It is the responsibility of this department to make sure that all working environments meet certain qualifications for safety. They are also the first department called upon when a work related incident is reported.

Quality Control and Wrapping

The department of **Quality Control** insures the quality of each product manufactured inside and outside the North Pole. If a product is not up to code, or is unmarketable, they set about either reforming the product, or sending fore replacements. If the product does not have their seal of approval, it is not distributed.

The **Wrapping Department** is in charge of gift-wrapping all items intended for distribution on Christmas Eve. They also package items to be shipped to various regions of the NPO, generally for export purposes.

The Kitchen

Though not exactly a department, the Kitchen is a vital part of North Pole life, providing the needed nourishment for all who dwell within North Pole City.

Like a giant cafeteria, the Kitchen generally serves more nutritious and tasty meals than found in most human manned facilities. Each food item is prepared with the health and well-being of each elf, or human, in mind. All items served are fresh and are prepared in the most sanitary method possible.

The Kitchen distributes food to the various regions via the Railway or, sometimes, using the Subway, but also occasionally by cart or sledge. They are able to produce ample enough food to feed several armies, should the need arise.

The various ingredients and foods used in the Kitchen are either grown in an NPO region or are imported from human habitations. The Kitchen is always open. And yes, they do serve hot chocolate and cookies.

Housing

Housing is extremely important to the inhabitants of any NPO controlled territory. There are several different types of housing available, dependant upon location and position.

For workers and normal citizens, including those in the Security League and related, several comfortable apartments are available in North Pole City and South Pole City. These apartments range from shared rooms to single occupants, to several rooms, depending on the preference and circumstances of each elf or family.

Each apartment is furnished with a comfortable sitting room, a kitchen, lavatory facilities, and anywhere from one to four bedrooms. Some models include other rooms that can be used as dens, workspaces, or storage. Each apartment also includes at least eight hundred square feet of space for the comfort of the tenants.

These complexes are often found in the middle of the city, and are easily reached from any part of the city, more often than not within walking distance, although the Trolley system does encompass the area. The complexes are generally four to five stories tall and include laundry facilities, both common and private.

The other housing facilities, reserved for those in managerial positions such as Santa Claus, include a suite of rooms in the Main Office Complex. These suites include a main sitting room, one to two bedrooms, a lavatory, and a small kitchenette. Tenants of these suites usually eat in the Kitchen located on the main level. The staff provides laundry services. These suites are located on the third and fourth floor of the building.

The Post

The Post is the postal service used by the elves to sort and stores any incoming mail for Santa Claus. It is also used for pouch mail communications between different elf settlements and corporations among the humans.

The Post is housed in a large, multi-storied building. It houses several different departments including: Incoming Departmental (ID), Outgoing Departmental (OD), Santa Mail (SM), Corporate Mail (CM), Observer Mail (OM), and Recycling (RC).

The ID is for all mail incoming from the different departments and is basically a mail sorting room. The mail collected and sorted in this department is then transferred to the OD where it is sent out or stored until called for.

The OM is for the creation and sending out of all letters intended for individuals, elf and human, who participate in Observation Duty. It is generally more for the humans that this department exists.

The CM department is for all mail dealing with corporations directly owned or controlled by the North Pole Organization, or who are in cooperation with the North Pole Organization and its affiliates. As most corporations are based in human habitation, receiving any other type of communication may cause suspicion unless sent via electronic mail (The Net), or through direct contact.

The RC is pretty self-explanatory. All letters that have served their purpose, mainly Santa Letters, are recycled and then redistributed through various corporations in the human world.

SM is for all mail intended for Santa, usually from children around the world. Not all letters addressed to Santa make it to this department, as some post offices are reluctant to allow Post employees into their dead letter departments, or they have already given the letters to someone standing in on Santa's behalf.

Every letter addressed to Santa, that makes it to North Pole City, is read, though not all are responded to. Such an activity would take too much time for even a large team of elves to accomplish and would never be finished. As is, the reading of the letters alone, and sorting of the letters into naughty and nice categories, takes a lot of time.

Each letter that has been addressed to Santa, however, is brought to the Head Elf's attention. The content of each letter is read, recorded, and then reported to Santa each night. If he is unable to read each report, one of his second in command steps in to do so.

Candy and Confections

The Candy and Confections department (C&C) is in charge of all candy and food production for Christmas delivery, as well as for the use of some outside corporations.

The department houses one warehouse sized building with three different levels. Each level is assigned a different department.

Level three houses **Production**, where all of all traditional candies and confections are manufactured. Level two houses the **Experimental Labs** and **Quality Control.** Level one houses **Packaging** and general storage of supplies. All finished products are transported to either the Export or Confection Storage, where they wait to be packed for Christmas delivery.

The C&C department is staffed by a work force of several hundred elves that work different shifts. Each is highly trained in his or her area, and follows a strict code of sanitation and safety to insure the highest of quality in all of their products.

Manufacturing

The Manufacturing department houses several other smaller departments: Toys, Mechanicals, Apparel, Electronics, Décor, and Miscellaneous. Each inner department has its own building and storage facilities.

Toys encompasses the production areas for all toy manufacturing, as well as the Workshop of Creation (WoC) where various new toys are created.

Mechanicals comprises the manufacturing of any product that uses general mechanics, such as bicycles, complex toys, and small electronics.

Electronics houses the creation of all electronic devices and toys, including small appliances, computers, and other complex electronic devices.

Apparel is in charge of manufacturing clothing of all types and styles.

Décor specializes in all items used for decoration, such as knick-knacks, including all fabric items such as curtains, table clothes, etc.

The **Miscellaneous** department specializes in all items not covered by the previously mentioned departments, unless such items are manufactured elsewhere and are imported. This might include novelty items or the like.

Imports

The department of Imports is in charge of keeping track of all imported items, those that are not made at North Pole City. There are many items that the elves do not make, such as store bought merchandise like most board games, sporting equipment, and other related items. Because they are unable to make all items requested, they must import those items.

Through a carefully controlled traffic process, the elves trade and purchase items that they cannot legally make because of patents, copyrights, and other considerations. These items are purchased from all around the world and require secure routes of trade.

The Imports department is scattered throughout the continents, with the main headquarters located in North Pole City. The items received through the separate Import Stations are transported via the Subway to various locations for storage, inspection, and quality control.

Exports

The department of exports is for the exporting of goods and other materials made in North Pole City, or from any city under their banner, including but not limited to the South Pole regions.

The Exports department shares similar webbing patterns to the Import department; being spread throughout all elf controlled regions. The materials are transported from the main Export building to various stations around the world, where they are then distributed between the various corporations controlled or allied with the elves.

Maintenance

Like all areas of high activity, a maintenance team is

necessary to ensure that everything runs smoothly. It is their job to make sure that every wheel is greased, every track is perfectly aligned, and that any and all buildings are kept in good repair.

Inside this department are the following sub-departments: Plant Maintenance, Housing Maintenance, Facility Maintenance, and Transportation Maintenance. Each sup-department is specifically trained in their given area to make sure factories, housing, transportation, and other areas are kept up to code.

Human Relations

The Human Relations department is in charge of instigating and maintaining all relationships with non-elves outside of the North Pole Organization, including business ventures, the setting up of Observer Partnerships, and other related incidentals.

The Legacy House

The Legacy House, or Santa's House, is the recognized home of the first Santa to inhabit North Pole City. Now, more of a museum, it houses the original furniture and artifacts of the first Head Elf of the NPO. Many elves travel from around the world to visit this historic site.

The two-story structure stands nearer to the outskirts of the city. Despite this, the house is well maintained, with a small staff of guides for those wishing a tour of the home.

MAJOR CITIES AND PORTS

North Pole City

North Pole City can be found in the middle of the Arctic Ocean, above Greenland but not entirely in the North Polar Region. It is an underground city, being encompassed about by a vast iceberg that has not moved in thousands of years, being firmly attached to the ocean floor.

Though the City is indeed under water, it is not directly even with the ocean floor. Instead, it is only several hundred feet below the surface. The iceberg that contains the city sits several hundred feet above the ocean's bottom, near the center of the berg. The berg itself, is several hundred miles wide at its most.

The most stable portion of the iceberg has been hollowed out like a giant snow cave, with the ceiling of the dome being within only a dozen or so feet from the top of the berg, enough to keep it solid enough on top for frequent traffic of sleigh teams and walkers. The top of the dome is about one hundred feet in diameter, with several smaller domes for various way stations and settlements.

Within the city are the various buildings described under the buildings section. Also within the city, aside from the housing district, are the Stables and various fields of greenery, as well as several small parks. Near the outer limits of the city are scattered exit points that lead directly to the upper levels of the berg and to the outside.

Despite common belief, North Pole City is not a frozen area where there is continual snow on the ground. It is only on the outer level that this atmosphere can be found. Within the city it is a different matter. Through the use of various technologies, as well as the principle of thermal dynamics, the city enjoys a fairly moderate climate, being neither too hot nor too cold.

The Stables, the Sleigh, and the Reindeer

The Stables include the pasture area for the reindeer and the barns where they are housed. There are around 25 different reindeer that are capable of pulling Santa's Sleigh, though not all are used in the team.

A team of reindeer generally consists of about eight to ten reindeer specifically paired for speed and strength.

Each reindeer has its own specific tack that is used during any flight, be it practice or practical.

The stables also host a highly trained team of veterinarians, who are always on call for the health and well being of all reindeer. Their job is to keep the reindeer in tiptop condition, mentally, physically, and, as odd as it may sound, emotionally. Without equal health in all these areas, a reindeer is considered unfit to participate in any flight.

Inside the barn, aside from individual and joint stalls, there is the tack room, an examining room, and a training room for the elves to learn either how to care for or fly the reindeer.

Of all of the upper management of the NPO, only three are given leave to drive the sleigh on any Christmas flights. These individuals include the HE, the HO, and the ERS. All others who may know the ins and outs of flying the sleigh do not drive unless it becomes absolutely necessity.

The reindeer are creatures similar to regular deer, with a slight difference in appearance. Their coats are darker and their antlers are shaped differently. They can pull or carry up to ten times their weight, a trait shared with the common ant.

According to ancient legend, reindeer gained their ability to fly from eating some magic corn seed. However, the truth is more complex. The specific species employed by the NPO are capable of displacing gravity, an actual element of mass. This ability to displace gravity allows them to use it like stepping stones, making it possible for them to basically walk on air.

The speed of the reindeer is something of legend. They must be capable of traveling faster than the speed of sound, and some think the speed of light itself, in order to make all of the deliveries necessary on Christmas Eve. Many scientists claim that it is impossible for anything to go that fast without complete decomposition of all elements and atoms involved. They do not take into account the variances in species and technology.

When the **sleigh** is in flight mode it creates an electro-magstatic bubble similar to the one used in the Subway. However, this bubble does not propel the sleigh. It merely protects it and the reindeer from the high speeds. It also cuts down on wind resistance and any other factors that may reduce speed. The reindeer alone are responsible for the propulsion of the sleigh. With the streamlined bubble surrounding them, all resistance is practically non-existent and their natural instincts kick in.

There is, however, a different element involved in making sure that all deliveries occur during the allotted time, not just factoring in the differences in time zones, which increase the amount of time Santa has to work in by several hours. Inside the sleigh is a small device that distorts time long enough for the sleigh to slipstream the time dimension and overcome the barriers associated with it. This is similar to breaking the sound barrier.

With this technology, it is no wonder that the NPO would have a Security League dedicated to keeping all outside threats to a minimum.

South Pole City
South Pole City is, in a way, an extension of North Pole City, in that it also houses all the major departments, only on a larger scale. The layout is also more akin to a grid layout, as opposed to the more wheel layout of North Pole City.

More warehouses are enclosed within this larger city, allowing for mass storage and greater production. A smaller Office Complex allows various members of the Leagues a place to work.

Ports and Way Stations
Spaced throughout the world, other smaller cities and stations have been created to offset the growing needs of

the NPO. Some of these exist as storage areas for items imported, exported, or merely for overflow. Other areas include farming and agriculture, thus helping to sustain the food supply of all regions under the NPO.

Some of the smaller cities are dedicated to the manufacturing of various products traded with those of the outside world.   Research facilities for Manufacturing, C&C, as well as for the Medical League, are housed in one of the smaller cities.

Ice Dome

The Ice Dome, also called "the Dome" for short, is the structure that keeps the whole of North Pole City intact inside the stationary iceberg where it is stationed. The Dome was created using advanced technology to manufacture a giant curved structure of ice over the whole of North Pole City. Due to the unique technology, the structure is able to handle the vast amount of weight placed on it by the icy layer above. (Think of the Dome as something like a giant snow globe, and you'd get it about right.)

Specifically manufactures struts are placed at strategic locations around the outside of the Dome to help maintain integrity. These struts, and the attached mechanical implements, allow various parts of the Dome to be opened for access to the upper layer of the berg. Smaller access tunnels also allow access to the upper layer as well. Such openings are often placed in areas of rough looking terrain to carefully conceal their existence. It is not uncommon for large ice sickles to form near such openings, some several feet in diameter.

A special tunnel was created for the sole purpose of allowing access to the upper layer via sleigh. This tunnel is accessed via the Stables and slopes gently upwards. A chameleon door, made to imitate the surrounding ice layer above, protects the opening. In extreme cases of emergency, vehicles of similar size to the sleigh may also access this tunnel. Such cases would include emergency evacuation and/or emergency maintenance on the Dome.

SPECIAL TITLES AND GROUPS

The Emergency Replacement Specialist and the Head of Operations

The Emergency Replacement Specialist, or ERS for short, is the only one given the authority to act in Santa's place should he become incapable of performing his delivery responsibilities. This role also involves such responsibilities as helping to keep the North Pole Organization up and running smoothly, working directly with the Head of Operations, and making regular inspection rounds of each department.

The Head of Operations, or HO, is responsible for the upkeep of all operations within the NPO, including but not limited to security, import and export, upkeep, construction and distribution, as well as acting as an aide to the Head Elf. He or she is sanctioned with the protection of the Head Elf as well as being his right hand man, though not as a personal bodyguard.

The HO and the ERS work hand in hand to make sure that everything is kept up to speed and in perfect order. They act as judges in any disputes not settled in private and are occasionally asked to settle disputes in private settings as well. They are also in charge of Observer Partner stationing around the world, including the pairing of Observing Partners.

The North Pole Council

The North Pole Council (NPC) is comprised of the Head Elf, the Head of Operations, the Security League Head, and the Emergency Replacement Specialist. This council is the highest level of authority inside the North Pole Organization. As such, they have final say on all decisions made in regards to the running of said organization, including laws, bylaws, and other matters.

This Council can act independently of the League Council, and has the authority to act in whatever manner is best deemed to protect the Organization.

Observer Partners

Observer Partners are part of a vast organization within the NPO that helps Santa in observing the humans around him. They act as his eyes and ears to find out who's naughty and nice. On occasion, they will also act as liaison or diplomat with Human Relations, helping to insure that their existence remains secret to the rest of the world.

Each partnership is comprised of one elf and one human, generally as closely matched to physical characteristics as possible. In the cases of direct physical matches, the human and the elf merely change places. Such partnerships are usually between human children as they seem to adapt better to different circumstances and are generally not taken seriously when they accidentally let slip their occupation. Most human children chosen for Observation partnership are between the ages of ten to sixteen.

Each applicant, be it human or elf, is chosen carefully and is fully screened for possible criminal history as well as other background information that might compromise the partnership. Only after a several sessions of extensive training are the partnerships allowed to occur. Without the passing of the training sessions, the candidate is rejected. Each session is scored and those who do not receive an adequate score are also rejected.

After training, the partners meet and a telepathic link is established between them so that they can communicate with each other, even if they are separated by thousands of miles. The elf takes the human child's place in society while the child comes to live at North Pole City, or one of its outlaying stations, trading off so that each has the opportunity to spend equal time with family and friends as well as working. The human child generally receives instruction in one of the many departments of the NPO.

On rare occasions, the Observer Partnering is between two elves, without the telepathic link created between them. The elf chosen for Observation Duty interacts with humans, blending in with the rest of society, and spending only several hours at one time in the public eye. They report directly to their partner who is generally in the upper management of the NPO who then reports to either the HE, HO, or ERS. Such Observers are sometimes called upon to spend longer spans of time within human habitation.

Recreation League

The Recreation League exists as a volunteer company to help maintain the mental and emotional health of all the inhabitants of any of the NPO cities or territories. Their duties include providing wholesome entertainment, maintaining recreational areas, and beautifying the environment.

ABOUT THE AUTHOR

Karlie Lucas is a preschool teacher and a member of the
American Night Writer Association and SCBWI. A
graduate of Southern Utah University, Karlie received a
Bachelor of Arts in Creative Writing. She is a member of
Sigma Tau Delta, The International English Honor
Society. She is interested in all things magical and
mysterious, especially elves and dragons. She currently
resides in the Dallas, Texas area with her husband.